UNINTENTIONAL PIRATE

DAISY EMORY

TURBO KITTEN

UNINTENTIONAL
Pirate

USA TODAY BESTSELLING AUTHOR CATHERINE BANKS
WRITING AS

DAISY EMORY

To Charity for being amazing and supporting me.

And, as always, thank you to my best friend and soulmate, Avery, for supporting me and being my rock.

CHAPTER ONE

"I won!" I yelled as I ran down the hallway towards the secret meeting room. My excitement caused me to enter the code wrong three times before getting it right, doing a fingerprint scan, and finally getting the four three-inch bolts to unlock with a loud "clunk."

Tapping my foot, I waited impatiently as the hydraulic door slowly slid open enough for me to squeeze through before I raced inside and waved the golden paper in my hand.

Five pairs of eyes looked up from the papers they'd been reading to see what I was waving.

"I thought you'd won everything when you found us?" Dane asked with a smirk and rotated slightly in his chair, draping his arm over the back.

"Well, apparently the universe felt I needed more," I said with a slight shrug, ignoring the fact that they'd heard me through the video surveillance and not just opened the door. I bet they enjoyed watching my growing frustration as I tried to punch in my code.

"What did you win?" Stephan asked with a soft smile that

didn't quite reach his eyes. He'd been staying up late in his office almost every night the past two weeks. He'd also been yelling on the phone, which was something he never did.

"I won a cruise!" I shouted excitedly, waving the golden paper again.

All of their enthusiasm died.

"Let me guess, Carnlial?" Forrest asked with a frown.

With a glare, I said, "I thought you would be more excited and supportive. Why are you acting so disinterested?"

"You know we own a yacht, right?" Arcadio replied dryly. His statement made me look at him and as I focused on his face, I noticed the scar. Despite the scar being barely visible, I could see it and it always made me cringe. Not because it took away from his attractiveness, no, it had only added to that, but because it reminded me that he had been hurt trying to protect me.

"That's not the same as a cruise ship," I countered. "I've never been on one and it's on my bucket list. I was hoping you'd all want to go with me, but if I have to go by myself, I will."

"Bucket list? You have a bucket list?" Dane asked.

"Yeah. Doesn't everyone?" I replied, my brows furrowing.

"What else is on your bucket list?" Stephan interjected.

"Why do you want to go on a cruise? They're always super crowded, have only tolerable food, and are expensive." Shea's tone held no inflection, so it didn't seem like he hated them, just that he was stating facts.

I plopped down into my chair on Stephan's left, and dropped my head onto my arms atop the table. "This was not the excitement I'd hoped to share right now."

Stephan stroked my hair. "We're sorry. It's been a rough

couple of weeks. Do you want to come back in and start over? We'll be very excited this time. Promise."

"Wait, I just realized you suggested you would go on a cruise without us," Arcadio said. "That's totally not going to happen. Where you go, we go."

"Now I'm sad," I whispered. "You ruined my happy mood."

"Go on, go outside and come back in. We'll do this right," Stephan ordered me.

"No, I'm just sulking like a baby," I sighed, and raised my head. "What are you guys working on?"

Stephan slid an extra copy of the stapled documents to me.

The staple was too high, so it barely held the papers together. "I take it Dane stapled these?"

Everyone chuckled except Dane.

"We were in a hurry," he said defensively.

Giving him a wink, I focused on the papers and started reading.

It was a request for partnership from one of the other mafias.

Over the past few months, our family—the Moriarty Mafia—had grown considerably in both revenue and reputation. After we'd dismantled Holmes' Mafia group, others started taking us seriously.

"Their focus is drugs," I commented, reading the information provided. "They seem to make a decent profit, which worries me that they're selling to young kids, or getting low-income people addicted."

Sure, we were a mafia family, but that didn't mean we couldn't have standards on what we did.

Stephan leaned his cheek on his hand, elbow resting on the table and said, "Read page four."

I skipped ahead to page four and read the breakdown of

who they were dealing to. "Wow, you guys dug up a lot of information on them." I knew they were good at investigating, but this was a lot for even them to have.

"I've been taking classes," Forrest said with a proud smile.

Focusing back on the document, I read ahead before making any more comments. When I looked up, Stephan was still staring at me with his cheek leaning against his hand.

"So?" he prompted.

One thing I loved about Stephan was that he allowed me to voice my opinions even though I was so new to this and really not a full-fledged member yet. Sometimes, they shot down my ideas, but they were always quick to explain why and provide more insight into their dealings. "They've got more members than us and seem to be doing fine on their own. Are we sure this isn't a trap, or a way for them to get closer to us and use what they learn against us?"

He smirked, but quickly stopped. "That is a possibility, yes."

"Do we have a way to stop them if that ends up being their game?" I asked softly. Immediately, the arm I'd broken when our rivals, the Holmes', had tried to blow us up, started to feel hot, and I rubbed it.

Five sets of eyes tracked my movement and all of their jaws flexed.

Putting my hands back in my lap, I cleared my throat.

"Yes, we have several plans in place. In the meantime, we'll be watching them closely to figure out what their end game really is," Stephan said.

"Is there anything in their history, or rumors you've heard, to suggest you shouldn't let them partner with us?" I asked.

"Not really," he admitted, and shrugged one shoulder.

"Okay." I stood up. "I'll let you guys resume your discussions."

"Where are you going?" Shea asked.

"To accept my cruise," I said smugly.

Stephan straightened and held his hand out. "Let me see, please."

I set my golden ticket into his hand, which had the cruise information on it and tried not to fidget as I waited for his response.

He read it completely, even the fine print, and then set it on the table. He turned his chair so that he was fully facing me. "If you decline this, I will schedule us for a cruise on the line that I use for business trips for five days instead of three. It will have unlimited alcoholic drinks, five-star chefs cooking our meals, and all of us will attend it with you."

"How far out would you schedule it?" I probed, despite wanting to scream yes immediately.

He looked over at Dane who was already scrolling through something on his tablet.

Dane finally stopped, lifted his head, and said, "We could probably do next month. I'm sure they'd be more than willing to add us to their roster."

Stephan looked back at me and arched a brow.

I leaped forward, throwing my arms around his neck, and straddling him on the chair. "Thank you!"

He patted my back, chuckling softly. "You're welcome. I think we all deserve a vacation after the year we've had anyway. Plus, it will give us all lots of bonding time."

I stood, brushed my clothes down, and couldn't stop the huge smile on my face even if I wanted to. "I love you."

He smiled. "I care deeply for you as well. Now, go decline the cruise and let us return to our business."

I saluted him. "Yes, sir!"

As I walked away, he said, "See? She knows how to respond to me. You could all learn a thing or two from her."

"I wouldn't mind her jumping into my lap like that," Arcadio whispered.

After waiting for the door to secure again.

Despite the increased security around the grounds, the guys felt it was necessary to increase security inside the house as well. My near-death experiences had really done a number on them. That, and the fact that someone had gotten into the office and planted a bomb without Stephan knowing.

Stephan seemed to take it the hardest, somehow considering it his failure. He had purchased several gifts for me as a way to try to apologize, and while I wasn't complaining about the gorgeous purses and jewelry he'd given me, there really was no need for him to apologize.

I skipped down the hallway, up the stairs to the main floor, and headed to my room.

My room had been completely remodeled to allow for a bed I could only describe as family-sized since it could fit five people on it. Most nights, it was only me and one of the others, but there had been a few nights where there had been more.

Sitting down at my desk, made from the wooden planks of a sunken pirate ship, I sent an email to decline the cruise prize. They would pick a runner-up or just discard the prize and save the money on it. Either way, it was out of my hands now and I had a month to get ready for a trip that all of my guys would join me on.

It hadn't passed my notice that Stephan had said there would be lots of bonding time. I knew he felt bad that everyone had been working long hours lately and this was probably his way to make it up to me.

"I think we need to talk," Stephan said from the doorway.

With a squeak, I spun and glared at the country's most eligible bachelor. "Do you tiptoe to my room just to get that reaction out of me?"

He smirked and shrugged one shoulder. "The world may never know."

Spinning in my chair, I tugged my legs up, tilted my head back, and looked at him as I continued to spin in circles. "What is it that we need to talk about?"

He stepped into my room, shut the door behind him, locked it, and crossed his arms over his chest. "First of all, you still need a punishment from when you disobeyed me."

Despite not knowing him that long, I had no fear of being locked in a room with him. My mouth dropped at his statement. "Seriously?"

"Yes."

"Fine, what are you going to do to punish me?" I asked. "And you'd better not say you're canceling the cruise because I just sent the company an email."

He smiled. "That would be far too cruel a punishment. No, that's not what I had in mind."

Now I was worried. I sat up straighter, set my feet down to stop spinning, and asked, "Okay, what then?"

"You're going to accompany me to a gala as my date," he answered.

"No!" I shouted, leaping to my feet in dismay.

He threw his head back as he laughed. "Yes!"

"Stephan, you know how much I hate those! Those women are so catty, and since you're the hottest bachelor on the market, they might even try to poison me just to get to you."

His smile dropped a bit and he stepped forward, setting his hands on my upper arms. "I'm not going to let that happen. Plus, it's a fitting punishment *because* you hate it, and I need a date. Would you prefer I took someone else?"

I dropped my eyes to his chest and mumbled, "No." He was asexual, but I still felt a connection with him. One that I didn't want him to share with another woman.

"As I thought. Now, the gala is in two days, so you don't have long to get a dress," he said, pulling out his credit card.

"I have dresses," I countered, but he gave me a glare that had my mouth snapping closed.

"Dane and Forrest will be taking you to get a new dress. Behave and let them pick out all the items you need. They know the most about this event and what style is required. You'll be leaving in about half an hour. Okay?"

I grumbled beneath my breath, but held out my hand for the credit card.

He placed the card in my palm before giving me a quick peck on the cheek and opening my bedroom door. "I'm suddenly excited for this gala."

"Excited for my torment is more like it!" I yelled, and only heard his laughter as he walked away. Truthfully, I was honored he'd asked me to attend with him. He could go by himself, and had on many occasions, so going with him was really an honor. I would hate dealing with the drama and the glares, but I would enjoy knowing I had been chosen to be at his side. It was also one of the few opportunities I would have to be alone with him without the other guys around. Stephan and I rarely got one on one time to talk and I wanted to get to know him better. Even though we weren't dating, we did live together and were friends, so it was important to me that we learn more about each other.

With just half an hour before the shopping trip, I quickly changed clothes and put on a bit of makeup. No matter how much I tried to doll myself up, the guys always outshone me and drew all of the attention.

I was okay with that, but hated when I drew negative attention. That tended to set the guys off and make them go into overprotective mode, and I didn't want to deal with the cops today.

"You ready to go, Babe?" Dane asked from the doorway.

I turned and nodded, sighing in resignation. "Ready as I'll ever be for a shopping trip."

He chuckled and held out his hand. "It'll be fun."

After linking our fingers together, I jumped up to kiss his cheek. "I always have fun with you."

"What about me?" Forrest asked from the end of the hallway, where he leaned against the wall with his arms crossed over his chest.

No matter how many times I saw these men, they still made my heart beat faster and my hormones pump harder.

With a shrug of one shoulder, I replied nonchalantly, "You're okay."

He smirked, grabbed my free hand, and jerked me away from Dane and against his chest. "If we weren't on a deadline, I would show you a fun time right now."

I made a purring sound and whispered, "Tease."

"Promises," he whispered as he bent down and nipped my earlobe.

I moaned and sagged against him. "So cruel."

"No shenanigans. Go," Stephan ordered from the speaker system.

I looked up at the nearest camera and stuck my tongue out at him.

"She does that again, you have my permission to take that tongue," Stephan said with a chuckle.

"Do it again," Dane whispered behind me.

With a shake of my head, I made my way to the garage and climbed into the black SUV with its tinted windows and bullet-proof glass. I climbed into the back seat and buckled my belt.

Dane climbed in beside me while Forrest took the driver's seat.

"So, do you know where we are going?" I asked.

Dane draped his arm across my shoulders and kissed my cheek. "We know where we're going."

I groaned. "That means it is likely a ritzy place I am going to hate."

"Hate is a strong word," Dane chided.

"Do you ever hate spending time with us?" Forrest asked as he backed the SUV out of the garage.

"No," I admitted begrudgingly. "Which is why I cannot wait for the cruise!"

"It is going to be really fun now that we're going on a *legit* cruise," Dane said.

I folded my arms across my chest and glared at him. "Legit? Ugh. You're so bougie."

"When you get used to the nicer things in life..." Dane shrugged without finishing the sentence.

I understood what he was trying to say. Since joining this group of guys, my lifestyle had completely changed, and I didn't like the thought of going back to what I had been. Secretly, I hid money in a savings account they didn't know about just on the off-chance that they kicked me to the curb, and I needed to try to survive on my own again.

"Hey," Dane whispered and tilted my chin up. "What are

you thinking about that has such a sad expression on your face?"

I smiled and shook my head, turning away from him. "Nothing. So, how many dresses are you two going to make me try on?"

"At least five," Forrest said.

"Times two," Dane added with a smirk that didn't quite reach his eyes as he looked down at me.

"What type of gala is this?" I asked.

"Political fundraiser, actually," Forrest answered.

"Oh, joy," I grumbled. Stephan *would* force me to go to a political event, my least favorite kind, for my punishment.

Normally, I would have gone to the mall near downtown, but since this was a high-end event that required a dress with a price tag higher than my yearly salary before I joined the Moriarty family, we went to the rich mall. Okay, that's not what it was called, but it was a small indoor mall with lots of security, stores that charged triple digits for a single pair of pants, and a food court that served caviar.

After parking and climbing out, Forrest took my hand and pulled me close to his side. "I feel like I've barely seen you the past couple of weeks."

I put my arm around his waist and nodded. "Yeah, you guys have been super busy."

"Tomorrow night, let's go on a date," he said.

"There's a new movie out we know you'll love," Dane added as he walked ahead of us to open the door.

"So, a double date?" I asked.

"Yep. Just Forrest, me, and you," Dane answered.

I walked by him and into the air-conditioned building. Two security guards nodded to Forrest and Dane as we entered, not bothering to use the wands to see if we had metal of any kind on us.

I waited until we'd walked a bit away from the guards to ask, "They on your payroll?"

"Yes, they're on *our* payroll," Dane answered.

Since I wasn't one of the big-wigs in the mafia, I didn't consider it mine. Though, since I worked for them, I guessed I could say ours.

"Are we going to eat here for dinner?" I asked, my voice a bit higher as excitement coursed through me.

Dane chuckled. "From the way you asked that question, it sounds like we'd better or you'll pout the rest of the night."

"I don't pout," I grumbled.

Forrest scoffed. "You're the queen of pouting."

"The others will be sad not to have dinner with you if we eat here, but they'll get over it," Dane said.

"Alright, now it's time for your least favorite activity," Forrest said as he stopped next to a doorway into a dress shop. "Time to try on dresses."

"Do I even get to pick one to try on?" I asked.

Dane and Forrest looked at each other and then back at me.

"Sure, you get to pick one to try on, but we still get to decide the best dress for the gala," Forrest answered.

"Why call it a gala if it's a political fundraiser?" I asked.

"Because the constituents are more likely to ignore when the politicians attend a gala or charity event than if they admit it's a fundraiser that only the elite are invited to," Dane answered. He stepped inside and immediately started looking inside the glass cases of accessories near the entrance.

I knew he wouldn't pick anything from the case because he had even pricier taste than this high-end boutique.

As if he'd heard my thoughts, he turned and both of them headed to a couch in front of two curtained rooms obviously for trying on clothes.

A tall, slender woman sashayed her way from the back to us. "Good afternoon, gentlemen. How may I assist you?"

"I need a dress for a gala," I answered, miffed she had completely ignored me.

Dane and Forrest smirked from their seats, but hid the smirks when she glanced at them.

She looked down at me, well over a foot taller than I was, and smiled. "I see. Do you have any color or style preferences?"

"Teals are my favorite," I said with a shrug.

She eyed me a moment longer, turned, and said, "I will bring dresses. Please go to the dressing room."

I mocked her silently, which got me more smirks from the guys.

At this point, I should have been used to being deliberately overlooked, but I wasn't. I wasn't super prone to jealousy, but I was very prone to irritation when they completely ignored me.

"Need help getting out of those clothes?" Dane asked and stood.

Forrest grabbed his arm and pulled him back down. "Shut up and sit down."

"Having sex in a changing room is on my bucket list," I commented, not really wanting to have sex right now, but wanting to tease them a bit.

"I need to see this bucket list," Forrest said.

"It sounds awfully fun," Dane agreed.

"I don't have it written down, but I suppose I could," I said. "There are a lot of items."

"Write it up so we can start marking off at least a few a year," Forrest ordered.

"Okay, but if I do, you guys have to make your own," I said. "And you have to make yours before I show you mine."

"That's blackmail," Dane said with a scowl.

I put my hand to my chest and dropped my mouth open. "Me? Blackmail *you*? Never."

"She's been around us too much," Forrest whispered to Dane.

CHAPTER TWO

"Inside, please," the woman instructed as she came back carrying several dresses in her arms.

I hurried inside and waited until she'd hung up the dresses before I started to strip.

Despite my initial dislike of her, she had picked some gorgeous dresses.

After sorting through them, being sure not to look at the price tags, I put on the one I hated the most, a fluffy monstrosity, so I could get it out of the way.

I stepped out of the dressing room and did a quick spin.

"Pass!" Dane and Forrest said immediately.

I nodded and went back inside to try on one of the others.

After trying them all on, I had a favorite and really hoped the guys chose it. They wouldn't let me see which one they chose, forcing me to leave the store completely while they purchased it, matching shoes, and who knew what else.

I stood outside the entrance, looking around at all of the rich men and women walking around in outfits that totaled at least four figures.

"Amelia?" a familiar, raspy voice asked.

I turned and my eyes bulged out of my head as I found my ex-boyfriend in an expensive suit with a gorgeous woman in an equally expensive dress on his arm. The dress was from one of my favorite designers, something easily recognizable due to their unique style.

"Trevor?" I asked. "What are you doing here?"

"I could ask you the same," he said, smiled, and walked over to hug me.

The hug startled me, but I returned it after a second. We hadn't ended on awful terms, but he'd seemed like he didn't have any interest in ever seeing me again.

"You look good," I commented.

He tugged at the lapels of his jacket. "Thanks. I got a job that pays really well."

Obviously.

"Where do you work now?" I asked.

"Husband, aren't you going to introduce me?" the woman at his side asked.

He smiled wide, put his arm around her waist, pulled her forward, and said, "Amelia, I'd like you to meet my wife, Ashton."

Married? The bum who couldn't be bothered to even look for a job, not only had a job that paid well, but was also married? Jealousy, fury, and a range of emotions burst through me, but I shoved them down.

I stepped forward, hand extended to shake hers, and smiled sweetly. "It's nice to meet you. I *adore* that dress."

She preened as she shook my hand. "Thank you. I was on a waitlist for six months to get it. Worth every penny."

"Amelia?" Forrest asked behind me.

Trevor tensed, his chest puffed slightly, and he straightened as Dane and Forrest approached.

"Dane. Forrest. This is Trevor and Ashton," I introduced.

Ashton's mouth dropped open. "You're the girl who joined the Moriarty group?"

I kept my smile despite wanting to scowl and ask what the hell she meant by that. "I work for Stephan Moriarty, though I'm not sure I'm the *girl* you're speaking of."

Dane and Forrest hovered at my back, and I didn't need to look back at them to know they were glaring at Trevor. I'd told them all about my deadbeat ex-boyfriend.

"So, are you a lawyer or what?" I asked Trevor with a smirk.

He laughed and shook his head. "No, I'm a broker."

"Oh," I said, even more surprised. "That's great. I'm so glad you found something you clearly enjoy and that pays well."

"Thank you," he said, his smile a bit tense now that the guys were with me. "I'm glad you found somewhere you are happy, too."

"I am happy," I agreed with a nod.

And I was. Happier than I'd ever been in my entire life.

So...why did I still feel so jealous looking at the couple before me?

"Well, I don't want to keep you," Trevor said. "It was good to see you."

"Good to see you, too," I replied. "Nice to meet you, Ashton."

She smiled, but her eyes were on the men behind me. "Nice to meet you all as well."

A new type of jealousy reared its head, but I again tamped it down.

She wiggled her fingers in a wave as Trevor pulled her away with his arm around her waist. Once they were a few steps away, their heads moved together and they whispered furiously.

"Honey?" Forrest whispered into my ear.

I squealed, leaped away from him, and held a hand to my pounding heart. "Forrest!"

He scowled, which was not the reaction he normally gave me. Where was his smile and laugh?

"What did he say to you before we got here?" Dane demanded.

"Did you guys buy the dress?" I asked, seeing their empty hands.

"Don't change the subject," Forrest said and folded his arms across his chest.

I got lost watching his biceps flex and might have drooled a little. "Huh?"

Dane stepped forward, took my chin between his finger and thumb, and tilted it up until we were eye-to-eye. "Spit it out or I'll go grab him and let Ox have him."

My eyes narrowed. "You're awfully grouchy." Realization hit me like a fly swatter to the face. "Oh my god, you're jealous!"

"Jealous of that loser? Psh," Dane released me and rolled his eyes.

"You are!" I squealed and laughed.

"Let's get some food. She's not going to spill until she's been fed," Forrest said and walked towards the elevators down the walkway from us.

"The green-eyed monster looks good on you," I whispered to Dane. "We should use that tonight."

He made a growling sound, but said nothing in response.

Once inside the elevator, Forrest hit the button for the

third floor, but then hit the emergency stop button between the first and second floor. He spun around, grabbed my hands, and pinned them to the wall of the elevator while his lower body pinned mine. "Tell us what happened."

"Or what?" I asked and licked my lips as warmth spread through me. "Will you punish me?"

Dane sighed, slapped a hand to his face, and let it run down.

Forrest bent down, lowering until he could look into my eyes. "Tell us."

I inhaled his scent, my eyes fluttering closed as it filled my nose and lungs. It wasn't pine or sweet, but it was one hundred percent Forrest.

His erection reacted and I pressed into it a bit, making him grunt.

"He didn't do anything wrong. I was just shocked that the bum who'd spent so many weeks on my couch was now wearing things I'd never been able to afford when I had my own business," I answered.

I opened my eyes and let Forrest see the truth in them.

He nodded and as soon as he loosened his grip, I pushed his chest and kicked the back of his knee at the same time, so he dropped to his back with a loud thud.

I pointed at his face, and said, "Don't try that shit again or you'll be clutching your family jewels instead. Got it?"

He smiled wide. "Our training is paying off."

I sighed, shook my head, and grinned. "You're incorrigible."

Dane pushed the button so we could finish the elevator ride. "That's part of why you love us."

He wasn't wrong.

Forrest stood, dusted his clothes off, and adjusted his

pants to try to hide his erection. "You sure we can't leave the elevator stopped a bit longer?"

I gnawed on my lower lip and looked up at him from beneath my lashes. "It *is* on my bucket list."

Dane chuckled excitedly and reached out to hit the button to stop the elevator again, but the doors opened and I ran out before he could stop me.

"Maybe next time," I said, and winked at them over my shoulder.

The food court in this fancy-schmancy mall was unlike any of the regular ones. Here, you went up to a style of food and ordered from a chef who would make exactly what you ordered.

There was Italian, Japanese, Chinese, Mexican, French, Cajun, and American, though American was rarely used.

"Too many choices!" I whispered and wiped at my mouth to make sure I wasn't drooling.

"You have three seconds," Dane said. "Three. Two. One."

"Sushi!" I shouted a bit too loudly, gaining the attention of almost everyone in the area.

Forrest chuckled. "Go find a seat and I'll order."

Dane draped his arm across my shoulders and guided me away from most of the people to an area where there were booths with higher backs. "Did you enjoy trying on those dresses a little?"

"Honestly, as long as I didn't look at the price tags, it was okay," I admitted.

He chuckled. "Stephan is going to be so excited to see you in that dress. I'm honestly anxious to see it myself."

"Why don't you have it?" I asked. "You're empty handed."

"They deliver it after making a few alterations to ensure it fits you properly."

"Oh." That did make sense. If you were paying so much money, you would expect to have it altered to fit you. "But she didn't even take measurements."

"She's a professional, Babe. She doesn't need a measuring tape," he said, releasing me so I could slide into the booth.

A couple of minutes later, Forrest joined us and sat on my other side so I was squished between them.

"Is fooling around in a food court on your bucket list?" Dane asked with a smirk, setting his hand on my knee, and slowly dragging it up my leg.

I smacked his hand and narrowed my eyes. "No."

He chuckled and moved a bit over. "Fine, fine."

"So, what's new in your world?" Forrest asked.

"Well, I found a new favorite pen. It glides across the paper like silk across lotioned skin," I answered.

"Is that why we got a huge box of one type of pen delivered to the building yesterday?" Dane asked with a smirk.

My mouth dropped. "My pens came and you didn't tell me?"

"I didn't know they were yours," he said defensively.

"How did you even order them?" Forrest asked. "Dane and I are the only ones who have access to the supply orders."

I whistled innocently and looked at the ceiling. "Wow, those are pretty chandeliers." They *were* pretty—and totally overkill to have in a mall, but then again it was a mall for rich people.

"Whose account did you hack into?" Forrest asked.

"Dane's," I admitted and looked back at Dane. "You've really got to find a better password naming convention. It's so easy to figure out."

His brows shot up. "You figured out my password?"

I shrugged. "It wasn't too hard. Getting access to your

computer was very easy."

"That's...I'm...dammit, Amelia!" he shouted and turned away from me. "That's overstepping boundaries."

I supposed it was since his password involved me.

"I'm sorry. Would it make it better if I told you that I think you're sexy, too?"

"No," he snapped and ground his teeth together, making his jaw flex. He stood up and walked away from the table.

"I haven't seen him pissed like that in a long time," Forrest whispered. "You might want to go after him."

I shook my head and blew out my breath. "No, he needs a minute to cool down."

"So, while he's cooling off, why don't you tell me why you were jealous when you saw your ex-boyfriend?"

I cringed. "Was it that obvious?"

Forrest set his hands on the table, leaned forward, and smiled at me. "Honey, I can read you like an open book."

With a loud sigh, I let my head drop. "It's not because I'm interested in him at all. It just hurt that he was such a bum when with me and now he's with a gorgeous woman, making a lot of money, and he married her. Was I really not worth the trouble? Not worth his time? Is she really so much prettier than me?"

Forrest sat back, but I dared not look up to see his face.

It wasn't often that I opened myself up to them to reveal some of my insecurities.

"Sometimes, even though the woman you are with is amazing, she isn't the right one," he began thoughtfully, obviously taking my concerns seriously. "She may be everything you thought you wanted, but something just doesn't click. Then, you meet another woman, one who fits you so much better and things just start making sense. You start wanting to improve yourself. To be better, do whatever you can to secure your future together. That doesn't mean the first girl was inferior, just not the right fit for you."

How did he always know what to say?

I looked up and smiled. "Thank you."

He scooted around the booth to put his arm around my shoulders and pull me against his side in a hug. "We had many women we thought were great, but then we stumbled into you and realized that you are *our* right fit. All those other women pale in comparison to you. Our souls are aligned." He dragged a finger down my cheek. "I feel more alive now than I ever have before. I feel like I *want* to live more now, too."

I grabbed his shirt and tugged him down to kiss him on the lips. "You should have saved that speech for when we were home," I panted.

He chuckled and kissed the top of my head before scooting back around the booth. "Sorry, fooling around in a food court is definitely not on my bucket list."

With a sigh, I stood. "I'm going to find Dane."

Forrest nodded. "I'll go get our food. I'm sure it's almost ready by now."

"What about your table?" I asked. "Won't someone take it?"

He tossed his jacket on the back and smirked. "Problem solved."

Trusting him, I headed in the direction Dane had stormed off to.

Although I could understand Dane was upset that I'd hacked his computer, I hadn't done it for nefarious purposes. I'd just wanted to order the pens and they'd been away.

Dane stood at the railing, looking down at the people walking around on the first floor. His shoulders were slumped forward slightly, his arms crossed atop the rail. His mouth was pulled down in a frown that had me swallowing hard.

I'd made him sad.

Walking up behind him, knowing full well he'd seen me approach since he never let his guard down in public, I wrapped my arms around his waist and rested my head against his back. "I'm sorry."

He turned around and wrapped his arms around me. "I'm sorry I snapped at you."

I shook my head against his chest. "It wasn't right of me to break into your computer. I could have just left a note on your monitor to order them for me when you came back."

"I'm not mad you figured out my password. I'm just..." he blew out a breath. "...sad. I had girlfriends who never trusted me and would try to get into my phones or emails to check up on me. They were always checking if I was talking to other women or cheating on them."

I hugged him tighter. "I'm sorry they did that to you. That's not what I was doing. I didn't even look at your files or emails or anything. I wouldn't do that. I just opened the browser for the supply orders and placed my order. Once I was done, I locked your computer and that was it. I trust you, Dane, and now that I know it upsets you so much, I won't do it again. I'll just leave you or Forrest a request next time. I'm sorry."

He sighed and leaned down to rest his head atop mine. "I forgive you. I just let my prior trauma affect my reaction to you. I'm sorry. Thank you for understanding."

Today was apparently an insecurity awareness day.

"Let's go eat," I said, lacing one of my hands with his.

He straightened and nodded. "Yes, let's eat before you start getting hangry."

CHAPTER THREE

Strong hands grabbed me and jerked me up out of bed, yanking me from a dream about some of my favorite male celebrities and me sharing a spa.

"Five more minutes," I mumbled as I tried to push at the chest of whoever was holding me.

"Wake up, Amelia!" Shea snapped in my ear, swept me into his arms, and held me against his chest.

My eyes snapped open. Shea never called me by my name unless it was serious. I looked around, but everything looked fine as we ran towards the safe room.

"What's going on?" I asked, wrapping my arms around his neck, and my legs around his waist so he could run, carry me, and pull his weapon as needed.

"Someone breached our gates, disabled the alarms, and cut the power," he answered just loud enough for me to hear.

Uh oh.

"Any clues who?" I asked, my mind going into preparation mode.

He shook his head. "I was ordered to grab you and get to the room with you."

"Wait, you were ordered to hide with me? What about the others?" I demanded.

"No more talking," he whisper-hissed.

I obeyed, my eyes scanning the hallways behind us as we ran, and any window we ran by.

We finally made it to the room and I exhaled a breath of relief to find everyone inside.

Dane hit the button to seal the door shut as soon as Shea ran inside.

"See anything, Ox?" Stephan asked, using Shea's nickname.

Shea shook his head. "No, Boss."

Stephan looked at me.

I shook my head.

Stephan nodded and turned to look at the wall where a large eighty-inch screen showed eight security cameras around the property. The front gate was open, a single black SUV had entered, and all of its doors were open.

Shea finally set me down and I walked closer to the screen, narrowing my eyes as I searched the cameras.

No movement on any of them.

Were they that good or were they hiding and waiting for us to make our move?

"They ran in, cut our alarms and power, and hid?" I asked and wrapped my arms around my stomach.

"Yes," Stephan answered.

"Why?" I asked aloud.

"We aren't sure," Dane answered. "We've been watching the screens, waiting for their next move."

Arcadio, aka the Jackal, sat in front of the screens, silently polishing one of his daggers.

I reached out and set a hand on his shoulder.

He turned his head and kissed my hand, his eyes never leaving the screens.

"There!" I gasped and pointed at the front door where two men wearing black tactical gear approached.

They pressed something against the front door and then disappeared into the night again.

Four people ran from the shadows around the house back into the SUV, backed out, and exited.

We waited, our breaths collectively held, but the door didn't explode.

"Think it's an invitation to the local church?" I asked with a smirk.

Four sets of eyes focused on me, scowling.

Shrugging, I smiled mischievously to cover my nervousness and quipped, "What? Nothing has blown up yet, and I'd like to go back to sleep now. I was just about to have one of the best dreams ever."

"Not yet," Stephan said. "We need to see what else they're going to do."

"They wouldn't have cut our power just to put a note on the door," Dane said.

"They would if they knew that we had installed turrets there," Forrest said.

"When did you do that, Flowers?" I asked Forrest, using his nickname.

"Two weeks after you were injured," he answered.

"We need to get the Sparkies out here to figure out a way around this situation," Stephan ordered. "I don't want to be defenseless just because they cut our power."

Stephan called our electricians "Sparkies" because he thought it was funny. The electricians didn't seem to mind either.

"I'm going to check the door," Shea said.

"Maybe we should approach it from the front instead of opening the door?" I suggested, swallowing the nerves I was hiding as I picture Shea approaching a possible bomb.

"I'm going to use the shield when I open it," he promised and kissed the top of my head.

"I'll go, too, just in case they left someone behind," Arcadio said, and stood. He kissed my cheek before following Shea.

Dane walked to the seat Arcadio had vacated, sat, and pulled me down into his lap. "They'll be okay. They're going to do it as safely as possible."

The desire to bury my face in his chest was immense, but I wouldn't look away from the screens, watching as Arcadio and Shea moved towards the door.

Shea had a large five-foot-tall shield in front of him as he walked. Arcadio walked just behind him, holding what looked like a spear.

Slowly, they moved forward until they were five feet from the door.

Arcadio leaned around Shea, extending the spear towards the door. The tip of the spear changed, becoming a claw that he used to twist the doorknob and pull it open.

He ducked back behind Shea, dropping the spear on the ground as the door opened. Shea braced his feet and leaned forward, preparing for an explosion.

Nothing happened.

Shea nodded once and Arcadio bent, picked the spear back up, hit a button that changed the tip to a pointed spear again, and carefully dislodged what looked like a piece of paper from the door.

The paper fluttered to the ground and landed harmlessly.

I let out a breath I hadn't realized I'd been holding.

Arcadio and Shea moved forward so Arcadio could stab at the item, poking and prodding it several times before they seemed satisfied.

Arcadio used the spear to shut the door and both waited a second, but again nothing happened.

Arcadio dragged the item with the spear closer to them across the ground.

"Easy," Dane grunted.

I looked down, realized I had dug my nails into his arm, and immediately released him. "Sorry."

He patted my thigh. "It's alright. Just breathe. They've been trained for things like this."

"Sort of," Forrest whispered.

Dane cut him a glare, but Forrest was staring at the screens.

I returned my attention to the screen, finding that Shea had set the shield against the wall and Arcadio had donned a mask and gloves before opening what appeared to be a letter.

He read it, then put it into a bag that he sealed.

Shea put the shield away, put on his own pair of gloves and a mask and started cleaning the area near the door where the paper had been.

"What is he doing?" I asked.

"Cleaning in case there's Anthrax or something on the papers," Stephan answered.

It had never even occurred to me that someone would put Anthrax or some other powder on the paper. This was why they were in charge and I did what they said...most of the time.

After a few more minutes, Shea gave a thumbs up and he and Arcadio returned to the room with the sealed letter.

"We've been invited to speak with one of the new mafia leaders in the next state, the Leonardos. They did this as an example of their abilities and to prove they're stronger than us," Arcadio said and tossed the sealed letter onto the table.

Stephan scoffed. "Yes, cutting my power definitely proves you're stronger."

"It proves we're too lackadaisical," I muttered.

They all looked at me.

Stephan arched a brow. "Something you'd like to say?"

Might as well be honest. I took a deep breath and then said exactly how I felt. "You're a tech mogul and you don't have a secondary power system or protections not tied to your main power grid. How do you not have some crazy invention not available to the public that would shoot a net or electrocute them or incapacitate them in some way? They could have blown up the house, or invaded, and we would have had to sit here hiding in the panic room like the sissy millionaires in those thrillers Dane loves to watch. It's pathetic."

Stephan smiled, which was not the anticipated reaction. "You're right. So, I'm putting you in charge of fortifying our house."

"M-me?" I stammered.

"Yes. The others will assist you in any way you want, but you get to fortify us with whatever gadgets and things you want. Shea will show you our secret lab for our tech items and Arcadio will show you the underground weapons laboratory. You can write down whatever it is you want from there or even ask one of the employees to design something just for you."

"You're going to let her get something designed?" Dane gasped and let his mouth hang open.

"Yes," Stephan replied.

"Spoiled brat," Dane muttered.

I preened and smiled wide. "Sounds like fun!"

"So, are you going to meet with these pompous jerks?" Arcadio asked as he spun his knife on the table.

"I'll agree to a video meeting first to determine their intent," Stephan said. "I'd rather not walk into any more traps."

"Can I go back to bed?" I whined. "I'm tired."

"Yes, but take one of them with you," Stephan ordered.

I giggled and rubbed my hands together. "Oh, exciting! Who should I choose?"

"No choice, I'm coming with you," Shea said as he stood from his chair.

"What?" Arcadio demanded. "Ro-sham-bo for it."

Shea glared down at him. "No."

Arcadio pouted at me. "Amelia?"

I shrugged. "Ox said I don't get to choose. Sorry, Jackal."

Arcadio sighed, and returned to spinning his dagger. "I've got to learn to speak up faster."

"Come on," Shea said and opened the door for me.

With a wave to the rest of the room, I followed Shea to my bedroom and immediately flopped down onto the bed.

Shea shut the door and then nudged me over. "Make room, Kitten."

I hissed, but rolled onto my side so he had room to lay down behind me.

His weight made the bed dip and caused me to roll backwards into his front, which he took advantage of to spoon himself around me.

"So, did you want to join me because you were worried about them coming back?" I asked softly.

He squeezed me slightly. "You know me too well."

With a chuckle, I patted his arm that had snaked around my waist. "I should hope so."

"We're all worried about you," he whispered.

"Why?" I asked, genuinely curious.

"It seems like you haven't been as happy lately. We were worried you might be having second thoughts about...us."

I couldn't hold back my laughter, which in turn made him pull away.

"What's so funny about that?" he asked.

"I've been worried that with how much you were all away from me, so caught up in meetings, that you were regretting being involved with me," I admitted to him.

He turned me onto my back and shook his head adamantly. "No, we've hated how much we've had to be apart from you. Even Stephan has been complaining and suggested that we bring you into discussions more. I think that's why he was so quick to jump on the idea of us going on a cruise together. It will give us all time to focus on each other and not the business."

"I think Stephan needs a break from all the stress he's been dealing with lately," I said.

"Agreed," Shea said and nodded against the back of my head.

"I heard him yelling on the phone the other night," I whispered. "It worried me."

"Yeah, it worried us, too. We brought him several drinks that night to calm him down," Shea whispered.

"Is there something going on that you guys aren't telling me?" I asked. "I know there's a lot of the mafia stuff you don't tell me about and I don't usually mind, but if there's something I can do to help, or lessen the burden..."

"We'll try to include you more," he promised. "For now,

let's just go to sleep. I started to lose my shit when you were in your room and those jerks breached our gate."

"You think we might need to move?" I asked. "So many people know about this place, especially since he holds parties here."

"You should mention that to Stephan," Shea said. "I've mentioned it, but he just dismissed it. I told him we shouldn't use our primary residence as a party place. He won't listen to me about that, though."

"I'll mention it," I promised and yawned.

"Tomorrow. Tonight, I'm going to sleep with you in my arms and know that you're safe." He pulled me snug against his body and kissed my cheek. "Good night, Kitten."

"Night, Oxie Loxie."

"You're withholding my pens from me because you're jealous that Stephan's letting me get new toys," I accused, put my hands on my hips, and glared at Dane as he continued typing on his computer.

"That's absurd," he said and scoffed. "I just don't know where your pens are right now."

"You said two days ago that they'd come in!" I argued.

"Well, someone moved them and I haven't located them yet," he replied.

"Someone named Dane," I said pointedly, with narrowed eyes.

"Children, behave," Stephan reprimanded as he walked out of his office.

He always wore suits, but today he looked exceptionally

handsome in a navy-blue pinstripe suit with a red tie. "Those pinstripes look great on you," I complimented.

Dane laughed bitterly. "Sure, butter him up."

I rolled my eyes. "I'm not *buttering him up*. He really does look good in that suit."

Stephan smiled and gently gripped my chin a moment. "Thank you, Amelia."

"Your next appointment is checking in with security right now," Forrest said, having sat by silently and simply observed Dane and I bicker.

Stephan nodded and adjusted his tie. "Good. I'm going to wait out here with you and look flustered and busy."

"You mean like every day this month?" I asked.

Stephan chuckled and his shoulders relaxed a bit. "Yes, I supposed I have been rather frazzled lately. I'm really looking forward to our trip."

"Me, too!" I exclaimed.

"Ready, Amelia?" Shea asked behind me.

We all turned to look at him and I scowled at the pretty woman in a very tight and short business skirt at his side. "Maybe."

"Play nice," Stephan whispered to me, smirking as he turned his back to hide his face from the woman.

She walked up and held out her hand. "It's a pleasure to meet you. I'm Anastacia."

"Nice to meet you as well, Anastacia," I replied and shook her hand, smiling professionally like I needed to.

"Anastacia is going to assist you with the orders you'd like to place," Shea explained. "She's our top inventor."

Anastacia blushed. "I wouldn't go that far, sir."

Sir?

"Down, girl," Forrest coughed at me beneath his breath.

"Stephan, can I talk to you for a moment first?" I asked.

He arched a brow, but nodded and waved towards his office.

I hurried inside and as soon as he shut the door I asked, "Don't you think we would do better to have a new primary residence that people didn't know the address for? So many people know our address and it's so easy for them to do things like last night and the attack when I was kidnapped. If our main residence was at a different location, one people didn't know about, it would be easier to keep it safe. To keep us safe."

He sighed. "Shea and the others have mentioned it, but—"

"You've been too prideful to listen."

He chuckled and dropped his head. "I was going to say stubborn."

"We can still stay at this place on occasion, but we really should find a better place to stay that's more secure," I whispered. "I was incredibly surprised to find out that the place you had parties at with well-known and easily tortured celebrities was your main house. You have so many enemies and stalkers and so few guards or perimeter walls. If you were a little more cautious, your life would be *a lot* less stressful."

He looked up at the ceiling and was silent a long time. I started to worry I had overstepped my lines with him when he finally spoke. "I don't know what it is about you, Amelia, but when you say things, I hear them better."

I preened a bit at that, but let him continue speaking.

"Fine, I'll allow us to find a new place. Actually, with how busy we all are, I'm going to put you in charge of looking for a new place, but I still want it fortified so do your research today and make your orders for two places."

My mouth dropped. "W-wait. You want m-me to choose your new house?"

"I want you to search and find your top three favorite places that are within my budget and size specifications. You will present them to me, and the others, with their pros and cons and then we will all vote."

"I can't," I whispered and looked down at my feet. "That's too big a decision to give someone who may not be..." I trailed off and blew out a breath. Why was I so negative lately? What was wrong with me? "No, I'll do it. You'd just hire some real estate agent who would only want bragging rights or to swap favors with another agent. I'll do it."

When I looked back up at him, he was scowling, but quickly smiled. "Great. Let me write down my specifications and then you can start your search."

When he handed me the list, I did a double-take at the budget. He was a very rich man, but I still couldn't comprehend so many zeroes right away.

"I look forward to your presentation," he said with a wink and then walked me back out to Forrest's desk.

"Ready?" Shea asked, scowling at Stephan.

I nodded. "I won't be placing all my orders today," I informed Anastacia. "However, I'd like you to show me everything you have so I can prepare my second order."

"Second order?" Dane, Forrest, and Shea asked simultaneously.

"Aren't these hallways a bit crowded for an echo?" I asked with a smirk. I winked at Dane and Forrest and headed towards the elevators with Anastacia on my heels.

The laboratory they took me to was straight out of a superhero movie. They even had a few Tesla coils in one of the rooms.

"Let me briefly explain one of our problems, then you can offer a solution," I said to Anastacia.

She smiled. "Excellent."

"We need a power source that can't be severed from outside. We don't want someone to be able to sneak onto the property and cut the power with no way for us to reactivate it."

"Oh, easy peasy," she said, walked to a nearby computer, tapped a few times, and pulled up an image of a metal box with what looked like pipes coming out of it.

I glanced at Shea who discreetly shrugged.

"This panel is installed in the basement or other hard-to-reach location within the house. It's hooked-up to this…" she hit a few buttons and a rectangular box with Stephan's logo appeared on it. "…which is a battery pack for lack of a better term. I recommend solar, but if you have other energy sources that you could use to store power, that works, too."

"So, even if the outside power is cut, this battery pack will have energy stored and allow our power to keep going?" I asked.

She nodded with a wide smile. "Exactly."

"Awesome," I said, and made a few notes on the tablet I'd brought. "What do you have in regards to panic rooms?"

Shea scowled. "There's already—"

I waved my hand, cutting him off. "I'll explain later."

He folded his arms across his chest and for a moment I got distracted by his very large biceps.

"I don't actually have much in regards to a panic room exactly, but I do have secure doors," she said and strode across the room.

Shea and I hurried to catch up to her and follow as she led us to a back area. There were several vault-like doors that reminded me of casinos. "They are designed to look like a vault, but we could alter the exterior to look more like a regular door or even conceal it to look like a wall."

"I'm not exactly sure how we'd want this one to look yet, but I do need the information on this," I explained.

"Can you give us a moment?" Shea asked. He gripped my elbow lightly, and steered me away from Anastacia and into a laboratory room no one was inside. "What is going on?"

I scowled. "What? I'm looking at the options she has available."

His jaw clenched and his fists clenched a moment as he stared at me in silence. "Are you leaving?"

My eyes widened. "What?"

"Are you leaving us? Are you...are you going to break up with us?" he asked.

I threw my head back and laughed until tears ran down my face. "What on Earth has you thinking that, Shea?"

"You're asking about a panic room for a house that doesn't exist. What else am I supposed to think? If I did something wrong, or one of the others, tell me. If it was one of the others, I'll beat the shit out of them until they can't walk or piss straight."

I took his hand closest to me and smiled up at the giant teddy bear. "Nothing happened. I'm not leaving."

"Then why are you acting like you're looking for things for a different house?" he asked.

I shrugged. "Because I am."

"You...don't want to live with us anymore?"

I sighed and ran a hand down my face before cupping his face and pressing closer to him. "Oxie Loxie, I'm not leaving. I'm just looking at things for a new house. I convinced Stephan to let me look for a new place as our full-time home."

His scowled deepened a moment and then his mouth dropped open. "He listened to *you*?"

With a frown, I dropped my hand and stepped back. "Why is that so hard to believe?"

"Years, Amelia. I have been asking him for *years* to either stop using our primary house as a party place or find a new one, and he refused to listen. One conversation with you and he gave in."

"Maybe you just wore him down and I was the last straw," I suggested with a shrug.

His eyes softened and he reached out to touch my cheek. "I think you getting hurt at his house was what did it. We all feel responsible for that night."

"Can we get back to Anastacia?" I asked to change the subject.

"One last thing," he whispered. "Will you go on a date with me tonight?"

I nodded, but then scowled. "Wait, isn't tonight the gala?"

He groaned. "I forgot about that. Okay, how about tomorrow night?"

I nodded with a wide smile. "It's a date."

He bent and kissed my cheek. "I can't wait."

We walked back out to Anastacia who looked at us in a calculating way that made me nervous.

"What do you have for security cameras and surveillance systems?" I asked her.

She scowled as she looked at Shea and then finally focused on me. "We've got the best in the world."

CHAPTER FOUR

After learning about all the inventions the technology department had, including several drones I was dying to test out, I was met at my office by Arcadio to take me to the weapons division.

We got into the elevator and he immediately hit the button to stop the elevator.

I looked at him expectantly, but it was several breaths before he turned, his expression serious.

"You know I care about you, right? A lot," he said as he looked down at me.

I smiled and reached forward to set my hand on his chest. "I care about you, too, Arcadio."

He stepped forward, pinning me between him and the elevator wall. "You're not leaving us, right? You're happy with us?"

My smile turned into a frown. "Why are you all asking me that?"

"You've seemed sad lately and it's made us all worry. Did you know we got into an argument and only Stephan stepping in stopped us? We started blaming each other and questioning what the others had done to you to cause it."

I reached up to cup his cheek, which he immediately leaned into. "I know I've been a bit all over the place emotionally lately. I'm sorry. I am very happy with you all. I love my life with you. I love my life here. Mafia hijinks and all."

"You swear you aren't planning to leave? Forrest said he found a savings account you've been sending money to secretly. One that you didn't even tell Stephan about."

I cursed beneath my breath and then chuckled. Of course they had found it. "I guess it's time for me to be vulnerable."

He waited patiently while I took a breath.

"I've been worried that you all might change your mind about me, so I've been sending money to a secret account, to ensure I won't be without money if that is what you decide, and I can find a new place to live. I haven't been reliant upon someone else in a very long time, so I wanted savings available to use if needed."

"So, you aren't planning to leave?" he asked.

I shook my head. "Not in a million years."

He smashed our mouths together and pressed his body against mine. After a bit, he leaned back and exhaled. "Thank goodness. I was getting ready to kill some guy who might be talking to you."

I laughed. "You thought I might be cheating on you?"

He shrugged. "The thought crossed my mind."

I laughed again and shook my head. "You really think I'm dumb enough to try to cheat on guys in a mafia? I don't want some poor idiot to get tortured and murdered because I couldn't wait or whatever reason I cheated for."

"You never have to wait," he said huskily and stroked a finger down my jaw. "We can do it right here, right now."

While the idea definitely had merit, I knew we didn't have time right now. "I'm sure any moment they're going to force the elevator to start moving," I whispered. "So, why don't we put a pin in that thought and revisit it later?"

He groaned and stepped back. "Right. Right."

On cue, the elevator started descending again.

Arcadio raised his hand and flipped off the camera in the corner.

I laughed and smoothed my hair and dress. These men were going to be the death of me.

"Stop that," Arcadio hissed.

I looked up at him and frowned. "Stop what?"

He groaned and adjusted the front of his pants. "You were chewing on your lower lip."

Whoops.

"Sorry," I said, and shrugged.

The elevator doors opened and he put his arm out to hold them open. "After you."

Since I'd already tormented him a bit, I decided it was okay to torment him a little more. "Thank you. Such a gentleman." As I walked, I sashayed more than normal and ensured my hip grazed his erection as I passed by.

He groaned softly, but cleared his throat and followed me. "Such a good view," he whispered behind me.

I stopped at what appeared to be a solid concrete wall with a keypad. "Here?"

He reached around me, pressing his chest against my back and made sure I could see the code he input. "Here."

1-2-2-7.

The wall shuddered and then split apart to allow us entry. Inside was a weapons facility fancier than anything I'd ever seen in a superhero movie or even a villain movie. It was my dream come true.

I squatted down and huffed.

"You okay?" Arcadio asked.

"One second," I whispered. "Pretty sure I just creamed myself."

He threw his head back and laughed, the sound echoing around the huge room.

I fanned my undercarriage and stood, certain my face was red. "Okay, let's go." There were about a dozen people moving about the facility with several robots moving boxes from location to location. I still wasn't used to the robots, but they were highly effective and kept injury claims down. I was still waiting for them to develop a manservant robot with AI that I could order around, but not all dreams would come true in my lifetime.

"You sure we can't go back in the elevator?" he asked.

"Show me a few of the toys in here and we might need to," I mumbled as I looked at the nearest weapon, a grenade launcher that shot fabric nets. "Can I get this for use at home?" I asked no one in particular.

Several men turned towards me, brows raised.

"Oh, you want to try and capture us?" Arcadio asked and started spinning his favorite kunai, a dagger with a hole at the top he could spin around his finger. "Sounds like a good Friday night."

"Oh, I won't *try*. I *will* capture you," I said confidently.

He smirked. "Only one way to find out. Hey, Antonio, ship one of these to Mr. Moriarty's address?"

I sighed and shook my head. "This is why we need a new house."

"A new house?" Arcadio asked.

I waved my hand, dismissing the comment. "Never mind, let's focus."

"Oh, I'm focused," he whispered, his eyes zeroed in on my cleavage.

"Antonio, was it?" I asked the older Latino man near the table of the net launcher.

He nodded. "Yes, ma'am."

"You have turrets or other extreme home defense items here?"

He smirked. "I can see why you like her, Arcadio. Yes, ma'am. Right this way."

Arcadio winked at me, sheathed his dagger, and walked at my side as we followed Antonio to view the latest-and-greatest in home defense equipment.

After seeing all of the available weapons, making a billion notes, and planning a weapon creation meeting for the following day, I was beat.

"Lunch time!" Arcadio announced.

I sighed. "Thank goodness. I'm starving!"

"Where do you want to order from?" he asked and pulled out his phone.

I shook my head. "I want to go out for lunch. With you."

Arcadio's eyes widened. "With me? Like, alone, on a date?"

I nodded. "You and I haven't had much alone time lately and I know lunch isn't exactly a fun date, but—"

"It's perfect," he said. "Let's go."

"Shouldn't we tell—"

"I'll text them," he said and linked his fingers with mine. "If we go up there, one of them might try to join us."

He was right, one of them would likely ask to come.

"So, we're sneaking away together on a secret

rendezvous?" I asked with a smirk and leaned closer to him, conspiratorially.

"This would be easier at night, but I can still sneak you out a side door," he said as he spun to the left, and took me down a hallway in the basement I'd never seen before.

Truthfully, I hadn't done much exploring in the basement levels at all. Maybe I should start doing that? It would help with any emergency escapes we needed to pull off.

He stopped before a door with a keypad, typed in some numbers quickly, pulled me through and then hit a small tan button on the left of the inside of the door. Immediately, we started moving...up!

"This is a secret elevator?" I gasped.

He nodded. "It's one only we get to use."

"We, as in..."

"Stephan, Forrest, Shea, you, and me."

"Where does it lead to?"

"Every single floor in the building."

"What? I've never seen this on our floor." I'd extensively explored the floor my office was on.

"I'll show you after lunch," he said with a wink. "For now, I'm having it take us to the loading bays level. From there, we can sneak out the docks and to my favorite restaurant."

Feeling like a sneaky teenager, I let Arcadio lead me out of the building, through the loading bays, and out to a building I would have missed had he not shown me it. There was a simple sign that said *"Abuelito's"* and that was it.

Inside, it was decorated like many other Mexican restaurants, complete with sombreros hanging on the walls and mariachi music playing in the background.

Arcadio nodded to an older gentleman who stood behind a bar where a single patron sat. Without waiting for a server to seat us, Arcadio steered me towards a large booth in the back corner.

The older gentleman started making drinks, walked to our table, and set two large margaritas down, rims thoroughly salted. He looked down at Arcadio. "Usual?"

Arcadio nodded. "Double the order."

The man looked at me, nodded, and walked away.

I took a drink of the margarita in front of me and it was like it went from my mouth straight to my soul. I exhaled a breath, my shoulders dropped, and I relaxed back against the seat. "Divine."

"I come here frequently," Arcadio admitted after taking a drink of his margarita.

"Are you telling me that you get lunchtime margaritas and don't invite me?" I asked with a glare.

He chuckled. "Well, from now on you can come, too."

"I can't believe you were holding out on me. What other secrets are you keeping? You'd better not be going somewhere and eating garlic bread, too. Sneaking out at night and getting ice cream?"

He laughed and set a hand on my thigh. "I promise, I'm not sneaking out for treats without you. Aside from this place."

"How are you doing?" I asked. "We haven't had much time to interact lately. It seems like Stephan has you working later than the others most nights."

He nodded and stroked his thumb over my leg. "I've been doing a lot of recon missions. We're trying to get a good understanding of our territory and things that are going on our guys may not be telling us about. Also, keeping an eye on our competitors."

"Are people pushing the borders?" I asked.

He scoffed. "Constantly."

"What do you think about the invite the other night?" I asked.

"I think I want to cut their hands off," he whispered. "I can't believe they trespassed and cut our power."

"Honestly, it might be a blessing in disguise."

He arched a brow. "Come again?"

"Stephan is letting me search for a new house for us," I admitted.

He choked on the margarita he'd just swallowed and had to cough into his napkin several times before he could look at me. "Seriously?"

I nodded. "That's part of why I was looking at all those home defense items that wouldn't work for the current place. I need to find things that I can have installed at the new place, too."

He leaned back. "I love our house, but once he started inviting celebrities over, even to keep his cover, it made me nervous. I like to have my own place that no one knows about. It made me feel a little less safe."

"Well, now we'll be able to fix that," I said. "Assuming I can find something within his restrictions that we all like."

"I'm sure you can. If anyone can find something that will suit us, it's you. You know us better than anyone," he said with a smile.

I leaned over and kissed his cheek. "Thank you for your confidence."

"So, what have you been up to?" he asked. "While I've been sneaking around, what have you been doing?"

"Your friends mostly," I said.

This time, he spit out his drink.

Doubled over in laughter, I could barely breathe.

He quickly cleaned up the table and shook his head. "You're a brat."

"Sorry. Couldn't resist myself," I panted as I wiped my eyes. "In recompense, I'll tell you a secret the others don't know: I've been doing a lot of research on the other groups."

"Please tell me you mean virtually," he whispered.

I smirked. "Yes, mostly."

"Amelia," he growled. "Tell me."

"I went to a dance club in Torreto's territory. There were rumors that some women went missing from the club, but other rumors that they made the best drinks in the country and I wanted to see what was going on."

He slapped a hand to his face and sighed loudly. "Why did you go by yourself?"

"Because they would have recognized you guys, duh," I said and rolled my eyes. "But I didn't go by myself."

"Who went with you?" he asked, his hand lowering, a jealous glower on his face.

"My girlfriend, Erina," I answered.

He scowled and tilted his head sideways a bit. "Wait, isn't she the wife of the head of the Gregori Mafia?"

I nodded with a wide smile. "Yep!"

"I had no idea you guys were friends. How did that happen?"

"We met at that holiday party Stephan threw last year," I explained. That party had been a mixture of celebrities, mafia leaders, and utter drunken chaos. Some girls got hammered, stripped, and streaked down the street. Apparently, the video went viral and they earned a ton of followers and money from it. I wasn't sure how they made money from it, but didn't really want to ask.

"Honestly, I'm not sure how I feel about you being friends

with another mafia leader's wife," he whispered and then took a big drink from his margarita, chugging almost half of it.

"Stephan said he thought it was a good idea for me to make friends with the wives," I replied smugly.

"So, you and another mafia boss's wife went to a club in yet another mafia's territory?" he asked. "Is that supposed to make me feel better?"

"Torreto's wife, Marlee, and Erina are best friends and we sort of became friends, too," I explained. "And before you get all overprotective on me, I asked Stephan's permission first. He said he didn't want to tell you guys because he knew you'd freak out and demand to go."

"Did you find out if the rumors were true or not?" he asked.

"I did. The rumors about the delicious drinks were completely true and the disappearing women were true as well, but not because they were doing it. A biker gang had set up shop there and started trying to smuggle women out for a prostitution ring. Torreto's group put a stop to it."

"And you believe them?" he asked, leaned back, and scowled at me.

I nodded. "I do. They showed me a lot of evidence to back up the claims."

"So, do you have any other new friends?" he asked.

The older gentleman came back and set chips and salsa on the table. I immediately grabbed one, scooped, and ate it.

"So good!" I praised.

The man smiled. "I am Miguel, and this is my restaurant. You are welcome here anytime."

My smile widened. "Thank you, Miguel."

"Be careful of this one, eh? He's shifty," he said and tilted his head towards Arcadio.

Arcadio scowled. "Rude."

I laughed. "You're totally right and I definitely will. Thank you for the tip."

He nodded and walked away.

Arcadio continued to scowl. "Shifty? That's rude."

"You should take it as a compliment," I said. "If he didn't like you, he would have waited to say something to me until you'd left. Clearly, he likes you."

"Yeah. Yeah."

"I saw on the calendar that you're going out of town in a couple weeks," I commented softly.

He nodded. "Yeah."

"Recon?"

He nodded again. Ever since my kidnapping, he had started doing reconnaissance missions and even assassinations. Originally, I was the only one in our group who'd killed anyone, but that all changed when the Holmes's had kidnapped me and my men had gone into berserker mode. Now, their desire to keep me safe, to keep all of us safe, slightly altered their moral compasses. They weren't just murdering random people or hurting innocent people, but their desire to hold back when confronted was diminishing with each situation.

"Promise you'll stay safe?"

He scooted over and hugged me. "I promise."

Memories from watching him get stabbed when I'd been abducted surfaced and I swallowed thickly.

"Sweets," he whispered. "I will be safe. I will come home."

"I thought I'd lost you once," I whispered. "Let's not repeat that."

He chuckled. "Ditto."

I cleared my throat and pushed him away. "So, tonight, we should play some games. Like board games."

"Yeah? That sounds fun. We haven't played games in a long time."

"We should place bets, too," I said with an evil smirk.

His smile turned into a matching smirk to my own. "Oh, yes. One hundred percent."

"You can't let the others know that I gave you a heads up to start thinking of bets or they'll get mad," I said. They wouldn't actually get mad. They'd complain, but not actually be upset.

He drew an x over his heart. "Promise."

"Think Stephan will be able to play?" I asked softly. He'd been so busy that we hadn't had much time to do anything.

"Wait, isn't the gala tonight?" Arcadio asked.

"Shit," I groaned and let my head fall back against the booth. "I forgot."

"Tomorrow night," he said. "Since I'm sure you'll need a night of drunken fun to forget the boringness of the gala."

"Miguel!" I called, getting his attention from behind the bar. I raised my margarita glass. "Another, please!"

He nodded and started making it.

Arcadio chuckled. "You going to be able to work if you have another?"

"I need it to forget about tonight," I muttered and downed the rest of my margarita.

Arcadio laughed and I smiled. His laugh made me incredibly happy. If I could make the assassin laugh more, I would. Maybe I needed to start searching for jokes to use at random?

"I'll take the blame if anything happens," he said, and clinked his glass against mine. "Cheers."

The next margarita was even more delicious and our food

was orgasmic. When we returned to the office, I only stumbled once, and I blamed that on the uneven tile.

Shea arched a brow at me, but they were smart men and made no comment to me about it.

Once inside my office, I created an account on a free real estate app, input our search requirements, and waited to see what available properties would pop up.

While I waited for that, I went back through my notes about all of the weapons and home defense items I'd been shown. There were so many things that I wanted and yet I knew I couldn't get them all.

I would need to prioritize items for each location. For our newest location, I was going with the most lethal options. Moving to a place that no one knew meant we could ensure very few people knew our location, so if anyone tried to mess with us, we could use extreme measures.

Measures that would prevent kidnapping and other things from happening.

"Here," Dane set a cup of water on my desk.

"Thanks," I smiled up at him. "How did you know I was thirsty?"

He shrugged one shoulder. "You always chug water after drinking."

The fact that he knew me so well made me blush. "Thanks."

"So, did you have a good lunch?" He sat in one of the chairs in front of my desk and crossed his ankles as he put his heels on my desk.

I smiled, thinking of sharing Arcadio's favorite restaurant with him, and what a great time we'd had. "I did."

"Good." Something in Dane's voice made me glance over at him, afraid for a moment that he might be jealous of my lunch with one of the others. But his eyes held an unexpected soft-ness that turned my insides into goo.

I held his gaze, the moment filled with intimacy. "Dane," I whispered.

Something sparked in his eyes. "Yeah?"

A noise from out in the hallway startled us both, breaking the delicate moment. I cleared my throat. "Um, is there anything I should be briefed on before I go to the gala tonight?"

After a beat, Dane grabbed a pen from my desk. "Not real-ly," he said. He started clicking the pen. "Just don't give anyone information about us. There might be a few journalists in there pretending to be celebrities and politicians in hopes of getting a scoop."

"I don't plan on leaving Stephan's side," I admitted.

"Good plan," he said. "When you go to the bathroom, just be quick."

"Did you know there are net launchers in our weapons division?" I asked, glancing briefly at the order invoice on my desk.

He smirked. "Yeah, why?"

"I ordered one for the house," I said. "Arcadio challenged me to catch you guys."

"Oh?" He dropped his feet and leaned forward. "We having a game?" Some of the previous intensity returned to his gaze, and I shifted in my chair.

"We might," I admitted in a sing-song voice.

"Sounds amazing."

It definitely did.

"Tomorrow night, are you busy?" I asked.

He shook his head. "Nope."

"I was thinking we could play some board games and

stuff." I was hoping we shared the same idea as to what "stuff" entailed.

"Fuck yes," he said with a huge smile.

"Great!" I declared happily.

He stood, walked to the door, but paused. "Hey, Amelia?"

"Yeah?" I asked and met his eyes.

"Even if we did decide to break things off, which we definitely aren't, we would never just kick you out. We'd help you find work and somewhere to live. Just so you know."

My smile slipped a bit, but I ramped it back up. "Good to know."

CHAPTER FIVE

CHAPTER

"No. Ew. No. No, No. What the actual fuck?" My comments regarding the mansions available to purchase in our area were varied and had drawn the attention of all of the men in my life.

"What are you looking at?" Forrest asked as he crunched on an apple, his suit gone and a tank top with a pair of fleece shorts at least three inches above his knees replacing it. The outfit was making it hard to focus on his face or the laptop in front of me.

"Well, right now I'm looking at your thick ass thighs in those shorts," I muttered, realized I'd said it out loud, and smiled wide to hide my embarrassment.

He chewed on his apple with a smile, showing off his delicious dimples. "And before that?"

"Have you guys looked at the ridiculous things that are out

there? Did you know how many insane millionaires and billionaires there are?"

"Yep," Arcadio and Dane said as they entered the room, each carrying a plate of cheese and fruit.

"Where's my food?" I asked with a pout.

"You don't get to eat until the event," Stephan said as he entered the room in a pair of grey sweatpants and a white t-shirt.

"Why do you all look so tasty today?" I questioned, my eyes narrowed, and I felt like I was being tested.

Stephan looked down at his outfit. "This looks tasty?"

"Grey sweatpants on men is a known delicacy for women," I said and tried, but failed, really hard not to look at his package.

"So, what atrocity are you looking at currently?" Arcadio asked as he leaned over my shoulder.

I showed him the mansion that was covered in shag carpet in various psychedelic patterns.

"Ew," he said and moved away.

"Exactly."

"So, no luck yet?" Stephan asked.

I shrugged one shoulder. "I've found a couple, but the ones I *really* like aren't in this country."

He scowled. "I told you it has to be within this state, Amelia."

I waved my hand. "I know. I know. But did you know that you can get a castle in Scotland for what you want to pay for a measly mansion here?"

His eyes widened. "You're serious?"

I nodded, clicked on the favorite icon on my item bar, and turned it around to show him. "See?"

Forrest, Dane, Stephan, and Arcadio grouped around the

front of my laptop to look at the castle.

"That's a gorgeous castle," Arcadio said, awe in his voice.

"Maybe we need a vacation home in Scotland?" Dane suggested.

"That's not a bad idea," Stephan said as he took control of my laptop to look at the other favorites I had. "I've always wanted a castle."

"I just want to visit another country," I mumbled as I flipped the laptop back around to resume my search.

"Wait, you haven't left this country?" Stephan asked.

I shook my head. "Nope. It's the first thing on my bucket list: Visit another country."

"Oh, you got a package," Stephan said. "Sorry, I just remembered. It's in your room."

"A package?" I asked with a smile, closed my laptop, and jumped up. "From who?"

"Erina," he answered.

I squealed and ran to my room.

On my bed was a white, rectangular package with a red bow on it. I tore the bow off and opened it, squealing loudly when I saw the gift.

Last time I'd seen her, she'd promised to get me a thigh holster to match the one she had. It looked like a garter with lace and frills, but also hid a small blade and a tiny pair of scissors that were perfect for escaping from duct-taped wrists. She had shown me hers and when I had asked to take a picture, she'd promised to send me my own instead.

"Time to get ready!" Stephan called. "We want to make an entrance, but not be too late."

"Yes, sir!" I called back and pulled out the tailored dress that had been delivered that morning, laying it out on the bed.

"The makeup artists are here," Forrest said as he led two women into my room.

They smiled at me as they set up their equipment and waved at me to sit at the vanity.

After an agonizing twenty minutes of letting them apply dozens of products to my face, they'd made me into a beautiful seductress capable of seducing a millionaire, or billionaire if I was lucky.

Okay, maybe seductress was pushing it, but they had transformed me into someone I almost didn't recognize. It was amazing and I loved it so much.

"You sure you can't just live with me and do my makeup every day?" I asked as they packed up.

They chuckled. "Sorry, but we can give you some tips if you'd like?"

"No, it's okay. I'm just being—"

"Herself," Dane answered behind me.

For some reason, I didn't want to turn around, to let him see me.

"We're finished," one of the women said as she took her kit and exited my room.

"I'm going to put my dress on now," I said. "Can you close the door?"

"Um, okay," he said softly.

Once I heard the door close, I glanced back, making sure he wasn't still inside. He had left, so I stripped and quickly put my dress on. For the life of me, I couldn't get the damn zipper all the way up, though.

"Zipper help!" I called out.

The door opened and I hid my face. "You got it almost all the way up," Dane said.

"It's so hard to get them zipped all the way," I muttered.

"Is there a reason you're hiding from me?" he asked softly, his warm breath brushing against my bare shoulder as he finished zipping my dress. One of his hands rested on my hip and I enjoyed the warmth.

"I know it's silly, but I kind of wanted to have you all see me at the same time."

He squeezed my hip once. "That's not silly. I'll go out in the living room with the rest of the guys."

"You're the best."

He chuckled. "Don't you forget it."

After he left, I double-checked my appearance and was surprisingly satisfied.

Raising my chin, I sauntered out to the living room and stood in the entryway.

Dane, Forrest, Arcadio, Shea, and Stephan all turned to look at me.

"Whoa," Arcadio exhaled.

"You look amazing," Shea said, his voice even deeper than usual.

"That is the most perfect dress for you," Stephan praised. He stood, walked to me, circled around a moment and stared into my eyes. Then, to my utter shock, he dropped to one knee, took one of my hands, and kissed the back of it. "I am truly blessed to have a woman of your beauty accompanying me tonight. Although I have a gift, it pales in comparison to you."

If my eyes could pop out of their sockets, they would have at that moment.

Stephan released my hand and pulled a thin, black, rectangular box out of his pocket. It didn't even have a logo or designer name on it. He opened it, revealing a stunning diamond tennis bracelet. It was something I had always wanted, but could never afford.

"May I?" he asked, taking the bracelet out of the box and holding it out towards me.

I nodded, too stunned to speak, and lifted the hand he'd kissed a moment ago.

He clipped the bracelet on and I turned my wrist this and that way to watch it sparkle in the lights.

"This is gorgeous and far too expensive," I said.

Stephan stood, set the box on the arm of the couch, and kissed my cheek. "Although you coming with me tonight is punishment, I felt you deserved a gift for not whining about it and working so hard this week."

"Don't question it," Forrest advised. "Just accept the gift."

"Come on, we've got just enough time to arrive fashionably late," Stephan said and opened the front door.

All of the guys stood and I looked at Stephan. "They're all coming?"

He smirked. "They're driving with us to the event, waiting nearby, and picking us up. Only you and I will be inside. Can't have someone see you flirting with my guards at the gala. It would spread rumors like wildfire."

"But I go on public dates with them," I reminded him.

He nodded. "I know. Look, I don't make the rules, I just know how the media works."

I shrugged. "Okay."

"I'm not sure I like this makeup," Dane whispered so softly, I was certain he hadn't meant for me to hear it.

I turned and arched a brow. "Why not?"

He cringed. "Um, well, you just don't look like yourself. I like your face."

"If I wasn't terrified of ruining my lipstick, I'd kiss you right now," I said.

"None of that," Stephan chastised. "Into the limo."

I paused and looked at the stretch limousine in the driveway. "A limo?"

"We always use a limo to take us to these events," Stephan answered.

"I've always wanted to ride in a limo," I squealed and quickly climbed inside.

"Did Stephan inadvertently cross something off your bucket list?" Forrest asked with a small smile as he climbed inside and sat on the far side of the limousine.

I nodded. "Yes."

"I still want to see your list. Are you ever going to show me?" Stephan asked.

"Apparently we all have to make one for her to show us hers," Dane answered.

"That sounds like fun," Stephan said. "Though, mine will be rather short."

Stephan had bucket list items? Now I was super intrigued.

"Can that be something we do this weekend?" I begged. "Share our bucket lists?"

Stephan smiled and draped his arm across the back of the seat behind me. "Sure. That sounds like fun."

"Might make Christmas easier," Shea said as he closed the door and then walked to the front to drive.

"That is incredibly true!" I gasped, not having thought of that before.

"So, remember to stay at my side all night, except for restroom trips, okay?" Stephan prompted.

I nodded. "Yes, sir."

"And don't call me, 'sir,' when we're there," he said with a shake of his head.

"What should I call you?" I asked. "Am I allowed to use a pet name?"

"A pet name?" he asked. "You have a pet name for me?"

"Maybe," I mumbled, feeling a little embarrassed to admit it, and looked out the window.

"But you've yet to tell me," he whispered and leaned close to me.

Had I not known he was asexual, I would have thought he was flirting with me.

"Maybe you'll hear it tonight," I said, turning and smiling wide at him.

He tapped the tip of my nose. "As long as it's not something super embarrassing, I will allow it."

"Are you sure you can't wear a wire tonight?" Arcadio asked from his seat beside Forrest's.

Stephan chuckled. "You all get to take Amelia out on dates from time to time without supervision. This is my time. Don't be greedy."

"If only this were a true date," I said and sighed dramatically.

Stephan scowled, his eyebrows drawing together. "Um, this is."

"What?" I asked, my own eyebrows scrunching.

"You're my date for this event; while it won't be all fun and games, this *is* a date, Amelia," he replied and tapped the middle of my eyebrows. "You'll give yourself wrinkles if you keep scowling."

Uncertain how to respond to that, I relaxed my face and sat back in my seat.

A date with Stephan Moriarty? Definitely not something I ever expected for myself.

"Oh, if you have weapons you need to take them off," Arcadio said suddenly.

I looked at him with a frown. "What?"

He pointed at my lower body. "You've got a garter on that you don't normally wear. I'm assuming you put a knife in it."

My mouth dropped. "How do you know that?"

"Well, once you told me that you became BFFs with Erina, and you got a package from her, I assumed it was like hers," he explained. "Connor and I do talk about things other than mafia business."

He was way too observant for his own good.

I opened my legs, pulled my dress up, and pulled out the small dagger. "Okay, you got me. But, can I keep the smaller one? What if I get kidnapped again and need to cut through duct tape?"

All of the men tensed, their shoulders rigid.

"You won't," Stephan said with certainty. "And they do thorough searches, so your scissors won't make it through."

"It's not metal," I explained. "It's ceramic."

"Oh, that will make it through fine," Shea answered from the driver's seat, the window partition down so he could hear us.

"Fine," Stephan said with a sigh. "You can keep the ceramic one if it will put your mind at ease."

"Thank you," I said.

"Give me your blade," Arcadio demanded.

"Don't lose it," I ordered him.

He scowled. "When was the last time I lost a blade, Amelia?"

I held out the blade, handle first, to him.

He took it gently, examined it, and smiled. "This is a nice blade."

"It's mine!" I shouted.

All of them laughed.

"I won't steal your new toy," Arcadio promised. "I'll just keep it safe." He tossed it up, caught it by the tip, and slid it into a sheath inside his jacket. He had at least six places for blades inside his suit jacket.

"Do I have to smile all night?" I asked.

"You can either smile all night or give everyone RBF, whichever you prefer," Stephan said with a small smile.

"I don't know if I'll be able to keep a smile up the whole time, but I'll try," I promised.

"No one is going to be looking at your mouth with that dress," Dane muttered.

I glanced down at my cleavage and smiled. "My cleavage does look exceptionally good in this dress, doesn't it?"

"I'm glad I won't be there," Forrest said. "I'd have to punch every single guy I saw for staring at your chest."

"Your poor knuckles would be so sore," I said with a frown. "Definitely not a good idea."

"That's what you're worried about? His knuckles?" Stephan asked.

"Yes."

He chuckled. "You are such an interesting person. I am going to enjoy my night with you."

My cheeks warmed and I looked at the window, sighing when I realized we had arrived. "Tomorrow night, we're playing board games together. All of us."

Stephan smiled. "Yes, ma'am."

The limo stopped, Shea climbed out, walked around, and opened the door.

Stephan exhaled and whispered, "Show time." He looked up, a smile on his face that looked charming, but I could see it didn't reach his eyes. He stepped out and then reached a hand inside.

I took his hand and let him pull me out.

Immediately, dozens of cameras started snapping pictures of us.

"Behave," Forrest ordered me from within the limo before Shea closed the door.

I resisted sticking my tongue out at him since I knew he could see me through the window even though I couldn't see him.

Stephan put my arm through his and we began walking down a red carpet with photographers on either side held back by metal barriers.

Some called out questions, but I simply plastered a smile on my face, kept my chin up, and walked at a pace even to Stephan's.

He stopped, slid his arm around my lower back, pulled me close to his side, and looked at a specific photographer. I looked in their direction and smiled as well.

"Who is your date?"

"Is she the secret wife that's been gossiped about?"

"Are you finally off the market?"

Stephan waved, took my arm again, and resumed walking until we were inside. The doors closed behind us and we entered an extravagant ballroom.

"Out of the frying pan and into the fire," he muttered.

I arched my brow and he chuckled.

"You're doing great. Let's mingle a bit and then we can take our seats and eat," he said.

"I am a decoration for your side tonight. Lead the way, sir."

He scowled for a moment, but a man with a woman

wearing a dress that showed twice as much cleavage as mine walked over and distracted him.

I realized I was staring at the woman's cleavage, so I jerked my gaze up and smiled apologetically at her.

She winked at me and placed a hand on the man's shoulder, laughing at something he said to Stephan.

Stephan slid his arm around my lower back again, gripping me once, but his attention was focused fully on the man.

I refocused and laughed at the next lame joke he said.

Stephan steered us towards one of the bars. "Let's get a drink."

"Yes, please," I almost shouted.

He stroked a thumb over my side. "You're doing great."

"It's a pretty low bar, Stephan," I said in a hushed tone so no one would overhear me.

The bartender dipped his head to us. "What can I get for you?"

"Champagne for me," Stephan replied.

"Whiskey on the rocks for me," I requested.

Stephan glanced at me, shocked, as did the bartender a second before making our drinks.

"I didn't know you liked whiskey on the rocks," he commented.

I shrugged. "I prefer whiskey lemonade, but I figured that wasn't an option here."

"Add some lemonade to her drink, please," Stephan ordered in his boss tone and then turned to face the other attendees.

"Thank you," I said and moved a bit closer to him while turning to look at them as well. "So, is there anyone I should be careful of?"

He nodded and his brows furrowed. "All of the women your age."

I laughed, but he kept his serious expression on. "You're not joking."

He shook his head. "I'm not. You need to be especially careful when you use the restroom."

"Um, okay," I replied.

"Your drinks, sir," the bartender said to get our attention.

We turned, grabbed our drinks, and then began mingling again.

After talking to half a dozen boring people about politics and business, I was ready to claw my way out.

"How do you do this all the time?" I asked him.

He smiled. "It's a small price to pay to keep my business going and my family safe." He looked down at me and brushed a stray hair back into place.

"You...you consider me family?" I asked, my words caught in my throat.

A portly man with a suit jacket that was too small to fit around him waddled over, his cheeks bright red. "Moriarty!" he yelled, interrupting my conversation with Stephan.

Stephan smiled at him, but his smile was even more strained than it had been. "Senator."

My eyes widened. This guy was a senator? I didn't pay attention to the faces of the politicians, more focused on their policies, but his appearance wasn't what I would expect a senator to look like.

"I wondered if you would show up tonight or not," the senator said, swaying slightly on his feet.

He was hammered!

"I wouldn't dream of missing this gala," Stephan replied.

The senator looked at me, his gaze resting on my chest a

bit longer than socially acceptable. He looked up at my face. "Who is this? I haven't seen you bring her around before."

Stephan's hand tightened slightly on my hip. "Senator, this is my girlfriend, Amelia. Amelia, this is Senator Hanson."

I dipped my head instead of holding out my hand, not wanting him to touch me. "A pleasure to meet you, Senator."

"Girlfriend? You have a girlfriend? She must be something special to make a playboy like yourself settle down after all this time."

The look the senator gave me made the hair on the back of my neck stand on end. No thank you. Hard pass.

"She is. If you'll excuse me, Senator, I'm going to take my seat now." Stephan steered me around the Senator and to a table with his name in front of two chairs. There was no one else at the table, so once we had taken our seats, I turned to him.

To keep appearances, I set my hand on his shoulder and leaned in to whisper in his ear, "How come a senator can't afford a suit jacket that fits?"

Stephan threw his head back and laughed.

His laughter caught the attention of many nearby, which wasn't surprising because it was such a nice laugh.

"This is why I wanted to bring you, Amelia. You always make a dark situation feel bright."

I shrugged and leaned back against my seat. "I do my best not to take things too seriously." We were silent a moment, drinking our drinks and people watching. "Stephan, are you sure it's okay to tell everyone I'm your girlfriend? Not that I mind…"

"If you don't mind, then it's fine."

He didn't look at me when he said it, but he seemed so nonchalant about it that I let it drop. I would need to talk to him later, but part of me was incredibly happy to have him refer to me with such a title to such important people.

As the food was brought out, people took their seats to eat. I didn't recognize anyone at our table, but I recognized the glares from a couple of the women around my age aimed at me.

I returned their glares with bright smiles before absolutely devouring the food on my plate.

That earned me a few wide eyes from the other women who picked daintily at their food. It was too delicious for that nonsense.

Stephan had begun chatting with the man to his left and the need to use the restroom quickly surfaced now that my stomach was full. I leaned over to whisper in his ear, "Restroom."

He scowled, opened his mouth as if to say something to me, but the man said something to pull him back.

I stood, ensuring I was stable in my heels before making my way towards the bathrooms on the second floor. In front of the bathrooms was a crystal waterfall that fell into a rectangular tank with bright lights and designs made by the lights.

The waterfall only made my need to pee even greater. "Good thing there's no line," I muttered to myself as I hurried inside the incredibly extravagant bathroom. The stalls went floor-to-ceiling with no cracks between the doors which ensured no one could sneak a peek at you while you were inside.

There were six stalls and only three were occupied. Not wasting my luck, I hurried inside one to do my business. To my utter surprise, there was a small hook on the stall wall to my left that I could hang my dress on.

"I wonder what brilliant woman thought to demand this?" I whispered to myself.

When I stood at the sink to wash my hands and check my makeup, another woman exited a stall and came to stand on my right. She glanced at me, curled her upper lip, and resumed washing her hands.

Two new women came into the bathroom and made a beeline towards me.

Tall and thin, with platinum blonde hair, their makeup and luscious deep red lipstick was flawlessly applied. Their dresses, from a high-end designer whose style I immediately recognized, were ones I'd only ever dreamed of touching.

"Who are you?" one asked. She was a bit taller than her friend, but much taller than me, her boobs level to my face.

"I'm Amelia," I said and smiled. "And you are?"

"How did you manage to get a date with Stephan?" The shorter—but still much taller than me—friend asked.

"Sorry, I don't have time for girl chat right now. You can come by our table if you want," I offered sweetly and walked around them towards the exit.

"We are at your table!" The taller one screeched.

"Then I'll see you there," I called over my shoulder, not bothering to turn around.

A hand wrapped around my wrist and pulled me back at the same time another hand grabbed the same wrist to ensure I had to stop. "I'm talking to you!" the tall one snapped.

I pushed her stomach, making her stumble back a few steps, and then pushed the shorter one on her shoulder to force her away from me. "And I said I don't have time. Don't touch me again."

"You bitch!" the two women screamed as they rushed at me.

Instinctively, I spun to face them; unfortunately, my heel caught on the hem of my dress and made me stumble.

The taller of the two reached me first and shoved me in the chest. Already off-balance, I fell backward, careening dangerously into the waist-height railing barely separating the second-floor hallway from the floor below.

"Amelia!" Stephan yelled and reached out towards me.

I scrambled to grab the rail, but the spray from the waterfall had made the top too slippery to hold.

My body felt weightless as I tumbled off the second-floor balcony straight into the freezing cold water tank below.

CHAPTER SIX

I surfaced with a splutter, wiped the water from my eyes, and reached for the side.

Several people had rushed over and were trying to pull me out.

Stephan pushed them all away and pulled me out of the tank and into his arms. "Are you okay?" he demanded, his eyes wide.

"My makeup is ruined, isn't it?" I asked with a pout.

His scowl turned into a smile and then he laughed and shook his head. "I never know what to expect to come out of your mouth."

"Your suit is going to be ruined!" I gasped and patted his chest. "Put me down."

"It's just water, Amelia, but I will set you down since you don't seem injured." He set me on my feet and wiped beneath my eyes. "Just a little mascara running, but you still look great."

"Flatterer. I'm sure my hair is plastered to my head, adding to my drowned cat look."

"Let us go!" the tall woman yelled. "We didn't do anything. She fell!"

Stephan straightened, his serious boss persona surfacing, and looked at the security guards who were pulling the women down the stairs. "I'm pressing charges so get the cops outside to come grab the women."

"You sure?" I asked. "I'm not hurt."

He looked down at me. "They *assaulted* you; you could have been seriously injured or died if the fall had been slightly different."

This was his world, and he was right, so I just nodded. "Can we go home?"

He pulled out his cell phone, put it to his ear, and barked, "Now," into the receiver before hanging up. He took his suit jacket off and draped it around my shoulders. I hadn't realized I was cold and shivering until the warmth of his jacket surrounded me. "Let's go." He draped his arm around my shoulders, too, adding even more warmth, and walked me out of the room and outside.

The photographers were still there and immediately started snapping pictures and asking questions about what had happened.

The girls were being pushed into a police car at the curb before us. Not helping their case, they started shouting insults at me until the cop closed the door.

The limousine pulled up, Shea jumped out, and his eyes widened when he saw me. "Hospital?"

"No. I'm fine, Shea."

"Police Station," Stephan ordered and pushed me into the limousine.

Arcadio, Forrest, and Dane stared at me with wide eyes as

I scooted across the seat, but remained silent until Stephan closed the door.

Stephan sighed and dropped his head. "I warned you the bathroom would be dangerous."

I rolled my eyes and pulled his jacket tighter around me. "I'm getting a thigh-high slit in every dress I wear from now on so this can't happen again. I was only off balance because I stepped on it."

"What happened?" Forrest asked through clenched teeth.

Shea glanced at me periodically from the driver's seat.

Stephan was furiously texting on his phone, though I wasn't sure to who.

"Two women were pissed that Stephan told everyone I'm his girlfriend, so they tried to get aggressive with me. I was actually pleasant and said I didn't have time to talk and tried to leave, but they grabbed me. I pushed the tallest one away and walked out, but then she came out and pushed me. I'd stepped on my stupid dress, so when she pushed me, I fell over the rail and into the water tank."

"You were pushed over a balcony?" Shea roared and swerved a second before righting and gripping the steering wheel so hard it creaked.

"Easy," Stephan ordered. "She's not hurt."

"She could have died," Forrest snapped.

"I didn't, though. Remember, I'm a mobsterina, so even when I fall, it's gracefully." I cracked a huge smile, trying to ease their fury.

It worked.

Shea groaned and shook his head.

Forrest and Dane groaned.

Arcadio sighed and slapped a hand over his face.

Stephan smiled and said, "I think you've more than served your punishment."

I looked down at my wrist and then screeched, "My bracelet! Those bitches stole my bracelet."

"We will inform the cops and have them search the women once we arrive," Stephan said. "I'll also call and make sure it didn't fall into the tank."

I sniffled. "If we don't find it does that mean I have to add it back to my bucket list?"

Stephan chuckled. "You and your bucket list. No, I'll buy you a new one."

My mouth dropped. "No way! That thing was stupid expensive."

"Stupid expensive?" he asked with an arched brow.

We stopped at the police station and I sighed. "Can one of the guys run home and get me a change of clothes? I don't want to sit in these all night."

"We won't be in there long," Stephan said reassuringly. "They need to see you in your wet clothes; it's evidence. We'll give a statement of what we saw, mention the bracelet, and then be on our way. Our lawyer is already inside."

"Our lawyer?" I asked, my eyes wide. "I have a lawyer?"

"We have a lawyer, yes," Stephan said. "If he tells you not to answer something or interrupts you, just do as he says. I pay him a lot of money because he's the best."

"Okay," I agreed, completely out of my element.

It actually went by even faster than I thought it would, and we were on our way home in less than an hour.

On the way home, I hit the button for the sunroof in the back and stood up, closing my eyes and enjoying the night air blowing on me.

"I wondered how long it would take her to do that," Dane said with a chuckle.

"Just watch out for signs," Shea ordered me.

My eyes snapped open and I sat down. "I don't want to push my luck tonight."

"Good idea," Forrest said with a small smile.

After a warm shower, a comfy pair of pajamas, and a warm cup of tea, I climbed into bed and fell asleep. Despite getting knocked into a water tank, the night hadn't been awful. It made me want to spend more time with Stephan and learn more about his side of our business.

≈≈≈≈≈

"Pay up, bitch!" I yelled when Dane landed on my property on the Monopoly board.

He groaned and handed me one hundred dollars. "This isn't fair. I'm convinced she's cheating."

"Poor loser," I sang as I counted my money.

We all sat around the coffee table with snacks, drinks, and our money and property cards. Stephan and I were vying for the most properties. I could see why he was a successful businessman.

"I need a loan," Forrest said and took a big drink of his beer.

"No loans, just sell your businesses and get out," Stephan said.

"I'll sell it for some kisses," Forrest said with a wink at me.

"Sorry, but you're not my type," Stephan said and winked back at Forrest.

I doubled over in laughter.

"Can we play a different game?" Arcadio whined.

"Are they always this pathetic?" I asked Stephan.

He nodded. "Always."

"Look, I've got to finish this game and see who is better," I said.

"We all know it's me, so we can just play something else," Stephan said with a small smirk.

He was totally goading me, and it was one hundred percent working. "We're finishing this."

"I'm going to make more drinks. Everyone looks like they need a refill," Arcadio said.

"I'll help," Dane offered and followed him to the kitchen.

Stephan and I battled for a measly thirty more minutes, and somehow the bastard defeated me. It was like witchcraft.

"How?" I asked for the third time.

"So, what are we playing next?" Stephan asked and clapped his hands together with a wide smile.

"I think I need a break from the games," I admitted.

Arcadio handed me a new drink, a margarita of some kind. "Why don't you show us your recent mansion finds?"

I shook my head. "Nope, I am not showing anything else until my final presentation tomorrow."

"You're already prepared to do your presentation?" Stephan asked, eyes wide.

I smiled. "Yes, sir."

"Why not do the presentation tonight?" Stephan asked.

"I'm not ready yet!" I said, "My presentation isn't finished."

"She's making a slideshow, isn't she?" Shea asked Dane.

"Let's play a card game," I suggested. "I need to get better at poker and blackjack."

"Speaking of gambling," Arcadio said and looked at Stephan. "When were you going to tell us that you let her go into enemy territory, alone?"

Stephan shrugged. "It was up to her to tell you, if she wanted to. She ran it by me, ensured she had approval to enter their territory, and was with her friend and their security the entire time."

"Wait. Wait. What?" Dane demanded and stood.

"Buzzkill," I hissed at Arcadio.

He folded his arms across his chest. "They deserve to know."

"Yes, I went into another mafia's territory, hung out at my friend's husband's casino, and then came home with no issues or injuries. Not even a paper cut."

My phone rang and I stared at the caller ID a moment before answering. "Are your ears burning?"

"What?" she asked and then sighed. "Amelia, are you okay? You're all over the news!"

"I'm what?" I squeaked.

"Turn on the TV, chick."

I waved at the TV. "Someone, turn it on."

"You sure you're safe with them? You sure you don't want to come live with me?" she asked in a soft voice, likely thinking one of the guys might hear her.

"I'm fine, Erina."

The news came on, and pictures of me entering with Stephan in my pretty dress and then exiting looking like a drowned rat played as they told a story of me being assaulted by jealous women who stole my jewelry at a gala event.

"You looked hot in that dress, girl," Erina praised. "Sorry some jerks ruined it. Want me to put a hit on them? My men will do it."

"No, don't put a hit on them," I said with a sigh. "I appreciate the gesture."

"Seriously, what the hell, girl? You need me to kidnap you?"

"A kidnapping might be nice," I whispered, though obviously not soft enough since every pair of male eyes in the room looked at me.

"Girls' night?" she asked.

"Please," I squeaked.

"You can't bring them, though," she said. "Or it defeats the entire purpose."

"I will talk with Stephan and ensure that when I come for girls' night there will be none of my men tagging along," I said loudly and smiled wide.

"The fuck?" Shea asked and stood. "Stephan—"

Stephan raised a hand. "She's entitled to go spend time with her friends. I'll speak with Connor."

Dane stood and stormed off to his room.

Forrest sighed and went after him.

"Did I cause more drama?" she asked softly.

"How soon can you kidnap me?" I asked instead of answering her, which was answer enough.

She started whispering away from the phone speaker so I couldn't hear her, then Stephan's phone rang.

He looked at it, looked at me, sighed, and then walked out to the back patio to answer it.

"Dane's mad at me," I whispered.

"He'll get over it," she assured me.

"How do you know?" I asked.

"If he wants to get laid this decade, he'll get over it," she said nonchalantly.

I burst into laughter and she joined me. This...this was why we were friends.

Stephan walked back in. "They'll pick you up at ten o'clock tomorrow morning."

"Aww, you took into consideration my need for sleep. You really are my best friend," I said.

Erina chuckled. "That and I want to get some before they leave to get you."

"Ew, TMI, bitch," I said, though I didn't really mean it.

"Whatever, I'll give you all the *juicy* deets when we get you."

I faked gagging, but ended up laughing with her.

"Bye!" I said and hung up after she said bye as well.

"I don't like this," Shea said softly. "They're our enemies."

"No, they're not," I said adamantly.

Stephan raised a hand to stop me from going on. "They are not currently our allies, but since our companions seem so keen on becoming friends, we are entering a truce and will most likely create an alliance."

"We can't ensure her safety if we don't send at least one of us!" Arcadio snapped and stood.

"You can't ensure my safety even when you're with me," I said and pointed at the television where a video of me walking out of the gala was playing.

Immediately, all of the men shut down and I bit my lip.

"Sorry, that came out wrong, but you know what I mean. I'm never safe. Not before you. Not now. Not here. Not with you. Not alone. Never. The least you can do is let me go have some fun."

That only made them more upset.

I groaned, sat on the couch and put my face in my hands. "Whatever, you know what, I'm tired. I'm going to bed and tomorrow I'm going to hang out with my friend. You all can accept that I'm going to continue being who I am and not a girl in a tower, or, you are going to lose me."

Arcadio's brows furrowed. Stephan frowned, but wouldn't look at me. Shea clenched his fists and then stormed out of the room.

Instead of furthering the discord, I went to my room and cried. Five minutes into my pity party, Dane snuck in, climbed into bed with me, and kissed my tears away.

"Don't cry, babe," he whispered as he spooned his body around mine.

The words were jumbled in my head and wouldn't come out properly. "Sorry. Emotions. Crazy."

He kissed my lips lightly to stop me. "It's okay. I just want you to know that it's not that we don't trust you and that we don't think you are capable of protecting yourself. We just always worry about you and would prefer at least one of us go with you to try to provide a bit more protection."

"I know and I really do understand. I just…it's hard to give up my control."

He chuckled. "You've been doing great so far. We appreciate all you've done and how much you've changed for us. You just aren't really used to the mafia life and you going into enemy territory is absolutely terrifying to us. They could use you as ransom or just kill you to start a war because they feel like it."

"Erina would never let that happen," I said adamantly. "And if she did, I'd go back and assassinate her, which she knows, so she won't."

Dane sighed and rested his head against mine. "It's hard for us to let go. You're the first…the first we've all truly cared about. The first we've truly…loved."

I looked up at him, my mouth open. "Are you...you're finally saying it?"

He got out of bed, turned the light on, and knelt before me. "I love you, Amelia. I love you more than life, more than coffee, more than anything else in the world. The thought of losing you hurts my soul, my very essence."

"I love you, too, Dane," I replied, tears in my eyes.

He jumped on top of me, pinning me to the mattress. "You swear?"

I nodded. "I swear that I love you."

His lips smashed into mine and he pressed his body onto mine, pinning me to the mattress. "I know that I don't own you on my own, that I'm sharing you with my friends, and I'm okay with this, but hearing you tell me that you love me..." He groaned and I felt his erection press into my leg. "I've never wanted to kill women before, but when I saw the footage of what they did to you, I considered it."

"I'm only upset that we haven't recovered my bracelet," I admitted.

"Two weeks, Babe. In two weeks, we'll be on our cruise and we can focus on just our relationship and fun. None of this mafia or political bullshit," he said and kissed my cheek.

"Wait, so soon?" I gasped.

He kissed his way down my jaw and to my neck, deliciously distracting me. "Yep."

I ran a hand down his back, gripping his muscles through his shirt. "Too many clothes."

He chuckled. "My exact thought." He sat up, pulled his shirt off, and I immediately ran my hands over his chest and stomach.

"Mm, muscles," I whispered and sucked up the drool from my mouth.

He pulled me into a sitting position and pulled my shirt off and then unhooked my bra in two quick motions. "Mm, boobs," he whispered.

I snorted a laugh, which quickly turned into a moan as he took my nipple into his mouth.

One hand held me upright while the other slid down my stomach to the pajamas, and pushed them down.

I lifted my butt up to help remove the pajamas and sharply exhaled when he dropped me to the bed and lay on me.

"You're heavy," I grunted and pushed at his chest.

He chuckled. "Rude." When he lifted himself off of me, I realized he'd been kicking his boxers off.

With no clothing hindering us, I wrapped my arms around his back, almost moaning at the warmth of his chest against mine, and kissed him deeply.

He reached down and with nothing between us, slipped his fingers between my legs and started rubbing my clit.

I stroked my tongue across his in time with his fingers and I came harder and faster than I had in years.

Dane pulled back from our kiss and arched a brow. "If you've been this worked up, you should have just jumped one of us."

I knocked his left arm out from under him, and rolled us so that I could lay atop him. Or that had been the plan, instead, I knocked his arm out and rolled off the bed and onto the floor.

He laughed as he looked at me on the ground. "I'd really prefer the bed to the floor. The floor hurts my knees."

I sighed, stood, and climbed onto the bed, pushing his chest so he laid down. "I was going for this, but failed."

He lay on his back, hands behind his head, and smiled

wide. "You can order me around, you know? I'm always happy to lay down and enjoy the view."

It took a little work to get fully seated on him, but once I did, we both moaned.

As I began to ride him, I ordered, "Say it again."

He gripped my hips, helping me move higher, and met my movements with thrusts of his own. "I love you."

My orgasm slammed into me like a tidal wave and I clamped around him, forcing him to stop his thrusts until it had passed enough for him to withdraw. He flipped me back onto my back and thrust into me hard, our skin slapping together.

"I love you, Amelia," he whispered, his mouth right beside my ear. He kissed my ear, my cheek, my throat, and my collarbone.

"I love you, too," I replied, my last word ending on a gasp as he bit my neck and started thrusting faster.

He dropped his head to my shoulder as he orgasmed and grunted, his body stilling above me and his breath ragged.

After getting cleaned up and redressed, I lay with my head on Dane's chest. "I totally kicked your ass at Monopoly."

He kissed the top of my head. "Yes, you did. Stephan totally owned you, though."

"Whatever," I grumbled. "I'll beat him one day."

"If believing that helps you sleep at night…"

I pinched his arm.

He laughed softly, rolled over, and draped his arm and leg across me.

"So heavy," I grunted and pushed at him.

"Shush," he said, but adjusted his position so he wasn't putting as much weight on me. "Mobsterinas need their beauty sleep."

CHAPTER SEVEN

"Give her to me!" Erina shouted with her hands on her hips as she stood in my doorway. Her wavy black hair was perfectly styled, per usual, and her dress drew attention to her perky and large breasts.

"Hello, Connor," Stephan greeted Erina's husband who stood behind her, smiling apologetically.

"Hello, Stephan. I apologize for my wife, but she's been very worried about her friend since she saw the news," Connor replied. He was tall, at least six feet seven inches, built like a swimmer, and had dazzling cerulean eyes.

Erina stepped around Stephan and threw her arms around me. "Hi."

I returned her hug and patted her upper back. "Hello."

She put her arm around my waist, spun so we were both facing Arcadio, Dane, Forrest, and Shea, who were all standing around the living room, and said, "You're all currently on my shit list."

All of their eyes widened.

"What did we do?" Dane asked.

"You made her cry for spending time with me. I am a good person. I am a good influence. You make her cry again and I'll steal her away and you'll never see her again."

I sighed, dropped my head, and shook it.

"I made it up to her," Dane said.

"Yes, I'm aware, which is why you're in a slightly higher standing than the others, but not much better," she said.

I groaned and looked at her. "You aren't supposed to tell him you know."

She shrugged. "My boys know I tell you and Marlee everything. If they don't want to be teased, they know to perform."

Connor's guard at the door, one of Erina's boyfriends and her husband's friend, chuckled and then coughed into his hand. He had the lightest complexion of the group and the brightest, fiery red hair I had ever seen.

"I apologize for asking you to allow me to meet you at your residence, but she was very insistent," Connor said.

Stephan waved his hand inside. "Not at all. Please, come inside."

"Show me your room!" Erina ordered.

I stepped to the side away from her, threw my hand up to my head in a salute, and said, "Yes, ma'am!" As I walked down the hallway, I marched with overexaggerated steps, my arms moving in time with each leg.

"Oh, I like this walk!" she said and copied me as she followed.

"It's scary how similar they are," Stephan mumbled.

"You're telling me," Connor replied. "You've yet to see them once they've started drinking and are together."

"We heard that!" Erina and I yelled back to them before I shut my bedroom door behind us.

"You haven't packed yet, have you?" Erina asked and folded

94

her arms across her chest, making her cleavage push out even more.

I pointed to my open suitcase with my swimsuit, socks, and bra. "I started!"

She walked to my closet, threw the doors open, and started grabbing stuff. "I'll help so we can leave soon. I want to get to the pool as soon as possible."

"You just want to get your boys in speedos and order them to serve us drinks," I teased.

"Oh! Speaking of that. Connor said you could bring two of your boys with you."

I tossed the pajamas I'd grabbed into the suitcase and blinked a second as I comprehended what she said. "Really?"

She nodded. "He and Stephan are likely working out their alliance stuff right now and since we're allies, you can bring guards with you."

Bringing two of them would be nice, but… "I'd rather have a real girls' night tonight."

She smiled wickedly. "Perfect! I already called Marlee and she's coming over, too. We're kicking my guys out, only my butler and chef will remain, and we're going to par-tay!"

"I get to pick the movies this time," I said adamantly.

She pouted. "Fine." The last time we'd watched movies, she had forced me to watch gory horror movies that I hid from most of the time. Hiding my face beneath a blanket didn't mute the sounds, though.

Once I'd finished packing, we returned to the living room where her four men and my five were chatting. Arcadio and the redhead of hers were showing each other daggers they kept inside their suit jackets. Forrest and another were comparing tattoos.

Dane looked at my suitcase with a scowl. "That's a pretty big suitcase for one night."

"I only have one size suitcase," I reminded him.

"Dane, be nice," Stephan chastised. He and Connor stood from the couch and faced us.

"We have confirmed our alliance. So, you are welcome to enter our territory and stay at our house whenever you wish," Connor said, his smile warm and welcoming.

"And the same goes for you, Erina," Stephan said, giving a similarly warm smile.

Erina clapped her hands together. "Great! I can't wait to visit you at your new mansion."

I elbowed her in the ribs. "Shush. They haven't picked yet. I'm showing them the choices tomorrow."

She rolled her eyes. "They're going to pick that one. I know it. They're stupid if they don't."

"Anyway," I said, drawing the word out. "I'm glad you two were able to form an alliance. And I appreciate your hospitality."

"May I take your suitcase?" the redhead who'd been comparing daggers with Arcadio asked.

"Thanks," I said with a smile and released the handle.

"You don't remember his name, do you?" Erina whispered in my ear.

I flinched. "Maybe."

She chuckled. "To be fair I only knew who Dane was thanks to his comment and our discussion this morning. We should make them wear name tags."

I looked at her, my mouth opened with a smile, and her mouth opened as well as our wavelengths connected. "Collars!" we said simultaneously.

"I see what you mean," Stephan said softly.

"Alright, say your goodbyes. We need to be on our way," Erina ordered me.

I walked up to Stephan who tapped the tip of my nose. "Behave and stay out of trouble." He hugged me and then pushed me towards Shea, who was the closest.

Shea pulled me into a hug, kissed the top of my head, and released me just as Arcadio pulled me into a tight hug and slid something in my front pants pocket. "Call if you need anything."

I kissed his cheek. "I'll be fine. It's just one night."

Forrest pushed Arcadio away from me to hug me, picking me up off my feet as he did. "Don't do anything I wouldn't do."

I chuckled and kissed his cheek. "So...free rein?"

He swatted my butt and shook his head. "You're incorrigible."

Dane squatted down until we were eye level and said, "Please be safe. I meant everything I said last night."

I kissed him lightly and whispered, "Don't worry, I'm the best mobsterina in the world."

He rubbed his nose against mine and whispered in my ear, "Love you, babe."

Erina grabbed my hand and pulled me out the door. "Bye, Moriarty boys! I'll bring your girl back tomorrow morning, dropping her off at work just like a respectable woman should!"

"I didn't pack work clothes," I realized.

She huffed. "The dress I packed will work fine. Come on! I want to get to the pool and get wasted!"

"I want that green drink we had last time," I said as we walked out of the house and climbed into the large black SUV she'd come in.

"Amelia," Stephan called out.

I leaned around Erina to look out the still-open door of the SUV. "Yes?"

"If anyone recognizes you from the news and tries to pester you, let one of the guards know immediately."

Erina smiled and blocked my view. "Don't worry, Stephan. My men will keep the public away from her. Only our family will be close to her."

Stephan nodded once and the SUV door was closed.

"Girls' night!" she yelled.

"Girls' night!" I yelled back and Connor immediately turned music on at a very high volume.

There was no doubt that my guys were worried, but this was a distraction I desperately needed.

"So, first we're going to eat lunch, okay?" Erina explained.

"At your house or a restaurant?" I asked, just for clarification.

"House," she answered. "We're going to spend our entire time at my mansion. We could go out in public, but honestly, things have been crazy for Marlee, too, so I'd rather we stay where we can ensure the public doesn't interact with us. Plus, your face has been plastered all over the news lately."

"It was very lucky that you landed in the center of that tank and didn't hit the edges," Connor said. "If I were Stephan, those women would only leave that prison in body bags."

"Did you find your bracelet?" Erina asked me.

I sighed and shook my head. "No. The women didn't have it on them and it wasn't in that tank. The only thing I can think is that someone else saw it at the bottom of the tank and snagged it." It really bummed me out that it was stolen.

"Stephan will replace it," Erina reassured me.

"It was so expensive," I hissed. "I don't want him to."

"Oh, she's like you were before!" the redhead said.

"What does that mean?" I asked and looked at Erina.

She smiled. "I used to complain about how expensive the gifts he bought me were before, too. I refused to accept a couple of them, but he left them at my house or in my room when I wasn't looking. You just learn to accept it."

"He's already paying for us to go on a cruise," I said and dropped my head back against the seat. "I'm still concerned about that trip."

"Cruises are fun the first few times," Erina said. "I'm sure your men will make it a great trip. When was the last time you went on a trip with them?"

My brows furrowed as I looked at her. "Actually, this will be our first official trip together."

Her mouth dropped open and her eyebrows shot up into her hairline. "What! You've never gone on a trip with them?"

"Well, we've flown somewhere to eat and play on the beach for a few hours, but we fly back the same day. I've never stayed in a hotel overnight with them."

"Oh!" she squealed and put her closed fists up to her mouth, hiding a huge smile. "It's a relationship milestone! Your first trip. This is so exciting. We have another task tonight now."

Whenever she said we had a task, it meant shopping. "I thought we weren't leaving."

"Online shopping," she said.

"For?" I held out the 'r' for a long time.

"You need the most perfect, jaw-dropping, sex on a stick dress we can find for the first night you go to dinner and dancing," she said. "I'm certain they've booked you on the same cruise line we use, they're the best, and they have these gorgeous ballrooms that you eat and dance in. All the rich snobs will be there, dressed in their finest, including single women looking to find a man for the night or the rest of the cruise."

"So, it's like the gala?" I asked.

She shook her head. "No politics, and people won't pester Stephan like they did at the gala. No, this is much better. It's your time to shine and show those boys they better put a ring on your finger soon or they'll lose out."

"How do you guys keep the tabloids from spreading gossip about your relationship?" I asked. Erina was married to Connor, but she was also dating the other three men with us in the car. Out in public, they did not hide their affection towards each other. "It wasn't an issue before, but now that Stephan publicly called me his girlfriend—"

"He did what?" Connor and Erina asked simultaneously.

I blinked. "You saw the news?"

"I saw them calling you his girlfriend, but they do that sometimes even when they don't have confirmation," Connor said.

"Well, yeah, when he introduced me to a senator and some other people, he told them I was his girlfriend," I answered.

"Did he ask you first?" Erina asked.

I shook my head. "No, but I told him it was fine."

"I need you to think very carefully," Connor said and leaned forward. "Did he, at any point in that same night, call you family?"

I nodded. "Yeah, why?"

Connor and Erina looked at each other and then Erina squealed like a school girl and slapped her hands against Connor's chest. He beamed, like a proud father.

"What is going on?" I asked, exasperated. "You're acting like teenage girls when giving juicy gossip."

"Sweetheart, we don't just throw titles out or call people

family who aren't," Connor said softly. "For mafia bosses, family is a title very few earn."

"Right, but I am dating his best friends, his guards, and living in his house. It makes sense to accept me as his family if his, basically, brothers are in love with me." I didn't know if they knew about Stephan's asexuality, so I didn't want to bring that up.

Erina scoffed. "You're so naïve."

I rolled my eyes. "The point is you're getting excited over nothing."

Erina and Connor exchanged a look before shaking their heads.

"We could hook you up with my designer," Erina said.

"Calm down," I said and chuckled. "There are plenty of gorgeous dresses not by an expensive designer."

She sighed. "We have so much work to do with you."

"I'm too sober for this conversation," I exhaled.

"It's eleven o'clock," the redhead said.

I narrowed my eyes and glared at him. "Thank you, Big Ben."

Erina cackled and slapped his shoulder. "Big Ben! Ha!"

"So, mimosas at lunch?" I asked.

"Whatever you want, boo," Erina said and patted my arm.

Their mansion was a thing of beauty with ten-foot electrified fences around the perimeter, guard dogs, and a security team that patrolled the borders constantly.

Once you made it through the gates, you had to drive up a long gravel drive around a water fountain, and to a set of stairs that led to a patio, and then to the double French doors. The house was brick and three stories.

They opened the doors for us and we walked up the stairs and inside.

An older man with slicked back grey hair and a slight hunch in a tuxedo bowed as we entered. "Welcome home."

"Jasper," Erina greeted. "You remember my friend, Amelia?"

Jasper smiled. "Of course. It's nice to see you again."

"Is lunch ready?" She asked him.

Jasper nodded. "Yes. It is on the back patio as you requested."

She clapped her hands together. "Wonderful. We'd also like some mimosas, if you could bring those out."

"Right away," he said, turning and walking off to the kitchen.

He moved surprisingly quick for an older guy.

"I'll take your bag up to the guestroom," the redhead said.

"Thanks, Big Ben," I said with a smile.

He rolled his eyes, but smiled as he walked away.

Erina looped her arm through mine and pulled me through the foyer, down the hallway, through a room that looked like it was never touched, and out to a patio that over-looked their pool and beyond that, their manicured gardens. "So, do you have any restrictions on the dress style?"

She was determined to help me find a dress for the cruise, and I wouldn't admit it to her, but I was glad to have some help.

"It has to have a slit up at least one leg. If my dress at the gala had, I wouldn't have lost my balance and that chick wouldn't have been able to push me over the railing."

"Oh, thigh-high slit is the best. Make sure you wear the garter I gave you."

The table was white painted iron with what at first appeared to be scrollwork, but when you got closer you realized it was depictions of skulls and hearts. Connor had custom ordered it for her as an anniversary present last year.

"Also, no pale colors," I said.

She dropped her chin down. "Do I look like an idiot? This is something you need to stand out in. It's going to be bright and bold."

On the table was a tray of assorted fruits, a plate of pastries, finger sandwiches, and chocolate chip cookies that she had delivered from thirty cities away each day.

Just as I finished adding my choices to my plate, Jasper returned with our mimosas. Not just two mimosas, but a pitcher as well.

"Thank you!" I said, grabbed my drink, and drank half. I exhaled and relaxed. "So yummy."

"Jasper, will you bring me my tablet, please?" Erina asked. "I started using my phone, but the screen is too small."

He dipped his head and headed back inside.

"Having a butler seems nice," I commented. "Not sure I could handle ordering someone around, besides my men, of course."

Erina chuckled. "You get used to it. Plus, I never order him. I ask nicely. It makes it easier to stomach. He also gets paid really well."

"So, when is Marlee coming?"

"Dinner time. She's helping her hubby with a negotiation."

"Is it weird that I almost prefer the mafia side to the business side?" I asked.

She laughed. "Not at all. I don't miss being part of the legitimate business at all. There's a lot more fun to be had on the mafia side. More dangerous and fun situations."

"I should add a gun range to our new place," I realized.

DAISY EMORY

"That way I can still play with the weapons when there isn't a war."

"Now that we're allies, it is very unlikely there will be a war," she said.

Erina and Connor didn't know about the incident at our house. Stephan wanted to keep it quiet until he met with them. I'd just told her we had someone breach our security and it allowed me to finally convince Stephan to buy a new house. It was the truth, just with a little omission.

Jasper handed Erina her tablet. "Here you go, ma'am."

"Thanks!" She replied cheerily and started typing furiously on the screen. After a moment, she turned it around and held it out to me. "Heart your favorites and we'll move on from there."

"Do you ladies need anything else?" Jasper asked.

"No, I think we're good for now. Thank you, Jasper."

He dipped his head. "I'll give you ladies some privacy." He turned, walked into the house, and shut the patio doors.

With one hand, I sipped on my mimosa and snacked on fruit and finger sandwiches. With the other hand, I scrolled through the dresses on the screen, tapping the heart icon on any I liked. "It might be faster to do a swipe left or right on these dresses."

"Oh, that's a great idea for an app!" she said. "You should ask Stephan about making one."

"You think others would use it?" I asked as I continued to scroll.

"Definitely."

"I have been looking for a new project that could earn some more money," I admitted. With a sigh, I handed back the tablet. "There, I favorited like forty dresses."

While she looked over my choices, I refilled our mimosas.

Staring up at the cloudless sky, I wondered if this peace might last for us.

"Hey, you never answered my question," I realized as I sipped my drink.

She took a drink of hers before looking up at me. "Which question?"

"About how you keep the media from making a big deal about you being in a reverse harem."

Her brows rose. "Reverse harem? Whoa, I guess that is what it is! Nice!"

"So?" I prompted.

"Let's just say that a few bribes and a few threats made our city's' journalists far less interested in our relationship. Plus, the fact that I married Connor and he doesn't hide that he shares—it makes people feel like it's more of a kink and they're embarrassed to bring it up. Honestly, I'd really recommend you consider marrying Stephan. Being his wife would bring you a lot of protection."

"I don't know if Stephan will ever marry," I said, trying to refrain from giving away secrets, which was hard because she was my best friend.

"People said the same about Connor and look where we are now," she said and smiled proudly. "You just need to show him your assets."

My laughter echoed off the back of the house. "He's seen my assets, though not in a sexual setting or anything."

"That's why we have to pick the perfect dress for this trip. Once he sees you in this dress, sees men drooling over you, and realizes that he doesn't want to lose you, he'll slip a ring on that finger faster than a virgin comes at a brothel."

Her analogies were always sexual and made me laugh. "I swear, your mind lives in the gutter."

"Alright, here are my top suggestions," she said and gave me back the tablet.

There were four dresses, each with thigh-high slits, and each with exorbitant price tags.

"Ignore the prices," she said, noticing my cringe.

"Fine. Fine." The dresses were gorgeous, definitely only to be worn at a gala-type event.

"Think of this as your Cinderella moment," she said. "This will be the time your men see you and think, 'Yep. She's the one. She is the woman I want to spend the rest of my life with.'"

"My Cinderella moment, huh?" I whispered. It was something I'd love to experience.

The guys had seen me in a few different dresses, but the one I was currently looking at was red carpet-worthy. Something an actress would wear. Something unlike any dress I had worn before.

I spun the tablet around and said, "This one."

She looked at the dress, her eyes widened, her mouth dropped open, and she breathed, "Yes."

Before I could turn it back around, she snagged the tablet, hit some buttons, and then squealed and kicked her feet above the ground. "Ordered!"

My mouth dropped. "What? You…what?"

"It'll be here in one week."

"Erina!" I squeaked.

She held up her glass. "Consider it a birthday present."

I knew there was no point in arguing, so I raised my glass and clinked it against hers. "I'll pay you back."

"Pay me back by slaying those boys in the dress," she said and winked. "And then share all the *juicy* details with me."

We laughed and drank our drinks. My heart felt a little bit

fuller knowing I had another person I could count on. One who could understand what it was like in the mafia world.

"Fine, but you have to agree to a Friendsgiving," I countered.

"Deal!" she shouted.

CHAPTER EIGHT

"In conclusion, I would suggest we purchase option one as it fits all of our needs and then some!" I said with a wide smile, ending my presentation of my top three options for the new mansion.

"Could you give us a moment?" Stephan asked, his hand steepled beneath his chin with his elbows propped on top of the conference table in his executive conference room.

His request surprised me, but I nodded, smiled, and said, "Of course." With my smile in place, I walked out of the executive conference room, shut the door behind me, and let the smile drop.

Why was he asking me to leave? He'd asked me to look for a house, so why didn't he want my input now?

"Why do you look sad?" Anastacia asked as she walked down the hallway.

I looked up and smiled. "Sorry, just thinking and it gave me RBF."

She chuckled. "I've got a problem with that myself. Had to train my brain to stop doing it at work."

"I don't think I could train my brain, it's like an old dog."

She laughed again. "You're funny. I see why they like you."

Before I could say anything else, she walked away.

The door opened behind me and Dane said, "We're ready for you now."

Why did I feel like I was walking into a job interview?

Instead of sitting in a chair at the table, I stood where I had been presenting the PowerPoint earlier.

"We have come to a decision," Stephan said, his hands folded in his lap as he leaned back in his chair.

I smiled. "Great."

"We have a place to show you and we need to hear what you think about it first," Stephan continued.

My eyebrows rose. "Uh, okay?"

Stephan nodded at Dane who took over using the projector and showed me a castle in Scotland.

"It's a gorgeous castle," I said, "but it's in Scotland."

"I want to hear what you think about the place, not the location," Stephan amended.

"It's beautiful, definitely one of my top picks, has enough rooms for us and many guests, and would be the perfect place for vacations with friends," I answered. "The cliff face would make for a perfect wedding spot, too."

Their eyes widened, so I quickly added to my statement.

"If we wanted to consider renting it out for such things when we weren't there. It does need security measures added to it, but it's stunning."

Stephan looked at me, his head slightly tilted as he thought for a moment. He often did that when I said something that surprised or confused him.

"Stephan?" Dane prompted.

Stephan cleared his throat and straightened. "Right, sorry. We will accept your top pick as well as the castle in Scotland."

My mouth dropped. "You're buying both places? You're going to own four locations then?" They also had a safe house that was rarely visited.

Stephan smiled. "I will be paying for these places, yes."

Shea opened his mouth, but Stephan cut a glare in his direction that had him snapping his mouth closed.

What was that about?

"Okay," I said. "Sounds good."

He clapped his hands together. "Great! Now, let's go home."

"Actually," Arcadio said and stood. "I'm taking Amelia on a date tonight."

"You are?" Dane asked.

"You are?" I asked at the same time.

Arcadio smiled. "We were going to go out last weekend, but the timing didn't work. Plus, we have the cruise soon."

"Speaking of the cruise," Dane said. "It actually got moved up."

"What?" I squeaked. "To when?"

"Four days," he replied.

Immediately, I bolted from the room and to my desk, my fingers tapping furiously as I messaged Erina. The dress wasn't due to be delivered for four days, which meant it was arriving the same day!

She called me and I answered immediately. "It's okay. They're delivering it to your place tomorrow night. Sorry, I should have told you it was arriving sooner."

I exhaled and dropped into my chair. "Thank goodness."

"How did the presentation go?" she asked.

All five men walked to my desk, scowling.

"Later," I whispered. I hung up without saying bye and smiled. "Sorry about that. So, do we have an agent we can call to work on purchasing the places?"

"Forrest is going to handle all of that," Stephan said. "Great work, Amelia."

"Thank you," I replied, a little shocked.

"My next meeting canceled, so did you want to discuss that project proposal with me now?" he asked.

I scowled, forgetting for a moment what he meant, and then gasped. "Right! Yes, please."

He waved his hand. "Follow me."

I skipped into his office, tablet in hand, and prayed Erina was right about this dress app.

⚜

Arcadio and I stood inside a cage, axes in hand, and faced the opposite end.

"You sure about this?" I asked softly.

He tossed an ax up and caught it in his hand without looking. "Definitely."

"You understand the stakes?" I asked, voice soft, body tense.

He nodded. "Do you?"

I nodded back. "Yep."

"Let's do this!" he shouted and threw his ax across the cage.

The sound it made when it hit was so loud that it echoed, even in the large room.

"A bit rusty?" I teased while Arcadio scowled. His ax had hit the wooden board on the opposite side, but in one of the outer rings.

"Let's see how well you do," he taunted, and tossed the second ax he held up and caught it, testing its weight more, most likely.

With laser focus, I stared at that bullseye, drew my arm back, and threw. The ax sailed through the air, end over end, and the tip buried into the board in the ring just outside the bullseye's circle.

Jumping for joy would be childish, so I just turned around, winked at Arcadio, and sashayed over to the little table where our drinks sat in the back corner.

"What the fuck?" he mumbled.

Arcadio had surprised me when he'd insisted on a date tonight, but he'd surprised me even more when he brought me to an ax-throwing bar. He was always full of the best surprises.

I sipped my whiskey lemonade and watched as the assassin grew still, his breathing evened out, and then he threw.

Bullseye.

"Impressive," I said, set my drink down, and returned to the line to throw my next ax.

He beamed, obviously pleased with himself, and walked around me, likely towards his beer. "That's what she said."

Laughter burst out of me, but I quickly tamped it down, focused, and threw my ax. It hit farther to the right than I'd planned, in the middle outer ring, but at least I still got points.

Arcadio tallied up the points for that round while I retrieved our axes.

"So, I realized that I don't really know much about any of your families," I said as I handed him his two axes. "Would you tell me about them, or a story about them at least?"

"My parents died when I was young and I bounced around foster homes, never really spending much time in the homes, so I didn't really have a family until I met Stephan," he said with a nonchalant shrug. "I can tell you a story about Stephan though."

I nodded and smiled wide. "Yes, please!"

Walking over to the line, he took aim and threw his first ax, hitting the ring just outside the bullseye. "When I first joined Stephan's business, he put me into self-defense classes. Not because I didn't know how to fight, but because there were a lot of basics I was lacking. Learning to fight on the streets doesn't tend to teach you basics."

"True, that," I said with a chuckle.

"At first, I threw a fit. Told him it was stupid and that I could handle myself just fine," he went on.

I could definitely see a younger Arcadio doing that. While he talked, I walked to the line and threw my ax, but my attention was more focused on him than the ax.

"Stephan made me a deal. If I could force him to his back only using my hands, not using weapons, and without fighting dirty, he wouldn't make me take the classes, but if he put me on *my* back, then I had to take them without whining. Being the cocky punk I was, I immediately took that deal. Stephan was young, thin, and just some rich jerk who didn't know what it was like on the streets."

"What happened?" I asked while sipping from my drink, fully focused on him.

Arcadio chuckled, admiration in his eyes as he met my gaze and said, "He tossed me on my back in ten seconds flat and as I stared up at the ceiling, defeated, I grew to admire him. It also made me realize that I couldn't judge every book by its cover. Sometimes, the big tough guys couldn't do anything but punch hard, and sometimes, the thin guys who rarely fought could hand you your ass within seconds."

"I could hand you your ass in seconds, no doubt," a guy said outside the cage.

Arcadio and I looked out at the cage's door where three guys stood, all sneering at us.

"Not interested," Arcadio said and took a drink of beer. "I'm just here to enjoy my date."

"Scared, little guy?" the biggest of the three asked. "Never fought someone bigger than you and won?"

"Oy, why don't you three piss off and let me enjoy my night? I'm trying to win a bet and your distractions aren't going to help," I said with a sweet smile.

Arcadio smirked as he walked by me to throw his next ax. "You're so sexy when you turn into our mobsterina."

"Oh, this your hustle? My bad, baby. If you finish up with him, I'll make whatever bet you want," the middle one said. He had slicked-back hair and a button-up shirt that was open halfway down the middle to show off his hairy chest. He looked like a skeezeball and I really wanted to punch his smirking face.

"You want to make a bet?" I asked and used my last ax to pick dirt out from beneath one of my fingernails.

"Oh, this is getting good," Arcadio whispered behind me. "The guys are going to be so mad they didn't come."

"A bet, huh?" the biggest guy asked. "What do you want to bet on, sweetheart? A kiss?"

"Sorry, my kisses are taken," I said with a smirk.

Arcadio draped his arm around my shoulders and smiled proudly. "All taken."

"I was thinking a monetary bet," I said, gave them all a once over and shrugged. "Unless you can't afford that."

"Name the stakes," the guy who hadn't spoken before then said. He was average height, dark hair, dark eyes, a face you would forget rather quickly if he blended into the crowd. His clothes were just jeans and a t-shirt, too. The way he stood, relaxed and yet seemed coiled up and ready to fight, reminded me of Arcadio. If I had to guess, he was the most dangerous of the group.

"Two rounds of ax-throwing each, which totals four axes thrown per person. Whoever loses has to pay two hundred dollars," I explained.

"So, you're potentially losing six hundred dollars not combined with your boyfriend?" the tall one asked with an excited smile.

"Yep," Arcadio said.

"Let's do it," the average guy agreed.

"Great!" I chirped and skipped over to retrieve our two already thrown axes. When I returned to Arcadio, I said, "Sorry, our bet will have to wait. I've got some money to make."

He wrapped his arm around my lower back, pulled me flush against the front of his body, and said, "I've got the rest of my life to make bets with you, Sweets." He kissed me and as our tongues clashed, I forgot we had an audience until one of them whistled. "Tonight, you're staying in my room," Arcadio whispered before we separated.

The desire to tell these men to forget the bet and drag Arcadio back to the house was near impossible to resist, but good things came to those who waited.

"I'm holding you to that promise," I growled into his neck before nipping it hard enough to sting, which made him moan.

"Temptress," he hissed and then walked to the other side of the cage so we stood on opposite sides with the first of our victims inside.

"Who do you want to play against?" I asked the big brute who had entered first.

"I think me and the tough guy will go first," he said, and winked me. "I can take you after."

I patted his shoulder as I walked by. "I'll play against anyone so long as they've got the cash in their wallet to back their talk."

"Damn, bro, that's how it is?" big guy asked Arcadio.

Arcadio shrugged. "I've spoiled her, and now she likes the finer things in life that cost a lot more money."

"Maybe I should ask for a raise?" I joked as I grabbed my drink and then walked out of the cage.

"He'd give it to you," Arcadio said. "We all think you need one, but you're the one who refuses to accept it."

My pay was astronomical compared to others in similar positions, but I wasn't going to bring that up in mixed company. I only accepted it when Dane told me to chalk it up to hazard pay for the mafia side of things.

"I'm going to get a refill," I informed Arcadio. "I'll get you one as well while you earn us two hundred dollars. That *might* cover our alcohol bill for the evening."

Arcadio blew me a kiss and then walked to the line to throw his first ax.

The average guy followed me to the bar. "I'll buy you this round, beautiful."

I smiled wide. "Sorry, but I'm already going to be taking your other money. I'll buy these."

We were technically on the outskirts of our territory, still within it, but right on the fringe, so I hadn't been to this bar before.

The bartender still hurried over when he saw us and to my

surprise, dipped his head to the guy beside me. "What can I get you, sir?"

Sir? Who the hell was this guy to be labeled a "sir" in our territory?

"The usual," he answered and gave me a smug smirk.

Ah, so he was a regular. That made sense.

"I need a whiskey and water and another Hop Mountain Ale," I said before the bartender could walk away.

The bartender looked at the guy beside me who gave a barely perceptible nod. What the heck?

When the bartender walked away, I turned and smiled at him, turning the charm on. "So, you come here often?"

He chuckled. "You could say that."

Something wasn't sitting right with me over this interaction, but maybe I was being paranoid.

A woman sauntered up, gave me a onceover, then set her hand on his chest and smiled. "Baby, where have you been? Things have been so boring without you here."

He smiled at her. "Business has been booming lately, so I haven't had much free time."

Business? Was he part of our mafia? A low-level or something?

I pulled out my phone and pretended to be looking for a signal so I could snap a picture of him and sent it to Forrest. I sent him a message asking if he knew the guy and if he was one of ours before sliding my phone back into my pocket.

"Well, why waste your time with messy chicks like her when you could have me?" she asked.

"Wow, you're pretty brash for a chick who works as a barista," I commented and turned to pour my lemonade packet into the whiskey and water the bartender had brought over.

"Excuse me?" she demanded.

I slapped a hundred-dollar bill on the counter, smiled at the bartender, and said, "Keep the change and keep the drinks double." With my drink mixed, I grabbed Arcadio's beer and headed back towards the cage to see how Arcadio was doing.

He waved four, one-hundred-dollar bills at me. "Hey, sweets! It's your turn."

I walked into the cage, walked right up to whisper into his ear, "I think they might be part of the mafia. I texted Forrest a pic of him to check." Louder, I said, "Here's your drink, babe! Great job winning. Who am I playing?"

"Me," the average guy said as he returned to us and walked right inside.

"Do your best," Arcadio said and kissed my cheek. He whispered before he walked away, "I'll research more."

I gave him a wink and then turned to the average guy. "Ready?"

He grabbed his two axes and nodded. "Yes."

I bowed and waved towards the bullseye. "Ladies' first."

He chuckled and walked to the line. "Cute."

"I hear that often," I admitted with a smile as I drank more of my drink.

I could see Arcadio out of the corner of my eye tapping furiously on his phone. The skeezy guy beside him was trying to peek at his phone, but Arcadio had a protector on his phone screen that made it hard to see it unless you looked directly at the front.

The thunk of the ax hitting the wooden backboard brought me back to the front where the average guy had hit the far outer ring.

Was he toying with me?

"Good job," I praised. "Points are points."

Walking forward, I threw my ax, narrowly missing the bullseye.

"So, have you ever been with a mafia boss?" he asked, his lips right next to my ear.

"I can't say I have," I admitted with a smile. "A few underlings, yes, but not a boss." That was all very true, but I still felt dirty for saying it.

"Well, it just so happens that I'm a boss," he said.

I turned and looked at him again. "Really? I would have pegged you for an assassin."

He laughed. "I used to be."

"So, what mafia are you with? Clearly not the Moriarty Mafia."

He spat to the side. "Those idiots have no idea how to run a proper mafia. They're too wrapped up in the skirts of their newest acquisition."

Was...was I the newest acquisition?

"Well, that is disheartening to hear," I said. "I heard they were a great mafia and came here to join them."

He looked over at Arcadio. "Is he one of them? Is that why you're here with him?"

Crap. I hadn't thought he'd look that way at Arcadio.

"I don't know," I lied. "I just thought he was cute and wanted to win some money off him this weekend. I thought, since he seemed like a killer, that he might be part of their group or at least know someone who was."

"Well, I can definitely find a place for you in my group," he said and sneered.

I bet he could.

"Sorry, but I'm not your usual mafia floozy. I've got some skills and won't be just another skirt to get wrapped up in," I said and winked before throwing my ax straight in the center of the bullseye.

His eyes widened when he saw the ax hit and he turned to face me. "Who are you?"

"Sweets, can you come here for a second?" Arcadio asked.

"Sure thing!" I called back. "Why don't you throw your next ax and I'll be right back."

Skipping, and acting like I didn't have a care in the world, I pressed my face into the cage so Arcadio could kiss me through one of the fence openings.

"They're part of the mafia who cut our power and—"

Before he could finish that statement, I turned, marched over to the average guy who had thrown his ax, grabbed him by the collar, and used my judo training to hip throw him to the ground. I pressed my knee to his chest and glared at him. "You're the asshole who woke us up in the middle of the night to try and what...scare us? You don't scare anyone, you average ass piece of crap!"

Arcadio grabbed me and pulled me back. "Easy, sweets."

"I thought you looked familiar," the average douche-canoe guy sneered. "You're the whore who's been distracting the Moriarty men with her supposedly magical pussy."

Before I could stop him, Arcadio stabbed a dagger into the guy's shoulder. "Watch your damn mouth."

I called Shea. "Extraction!" I gave him the address and then hung up.

"You just signed your death warrant," the giant guy said as he came into the cage with us, and punched a fist into his open hand.

"You take Goliath and I'll take the *boss*," I ordered Arcadio.

He smiled. "Aw, you're spoiling me tonight."

I winked. "Don't get used to it, baby doll."

He glared. "No. I do not approve of that nickname."

With a pout, I turned back to the boss who clutched his bleeding shoulder. "Can you believe him? I gave him a super cute nickname and he just flat out told me no? So rude. Anyway, did you know there's a knife sticking out of your shoulder? That looks super painful. Let me help you with that."

"No!" he shouted and stumbled back, but I darted forward, grabbed the hilt of the dagger, and yanked it out.

He screamed in pain, higher-pitched than even I could, and stumbled back until he slammed into the board where the bullseye was.

"Man, you are super dramatic. That is not a good look to have in front of your men. Just a word of advice," I said, and shook my head. "I could probably stab the Moriarty Mafia boss and he'd sniff like I smelled bad. You've got a lot to learn."

"I warned him," he snarled. "I warned him we would come after you all. This right here...this means war."

"War? You want a war with the Moriarty Mafia? Are you insane?" I asked and laughed loudly. As my laughter echoed around the room, it reminded me of one of my favorite anime villainesses and that made me incredibly happy.

My distraction cost me a slap across the face.

As my face whipped sideways, I realized Arcadio had watched the entire thing. He drew another dagger from his boot and stomped towards us, but the skeezball entered the cage finally and launched himself at Arcadio, stopping him.

At the door, I saw more men heading inside, ones I did not recognize.

Righting myself, I cracked my neck side to side and shook out my hands. "Now, you've done it."

The guy had begun limping towards the cage door but

stopped when I spoke. "You'd do well to remember your place."

"My place?" I asked and scoffed. "That's my line for *you*! This is Moriarty Mafia territory."

There were at least four men who'd come in, but just behind them, I saw Shea, Forrest, and Dane enter.

"You've got it twisted, *boss*. I know my place. It's at the Moriarty boss's side. You're the one who needs to learn your place." I grabbed an ax from the nearby table but stopped when Stephan yelled.

"Enough!" He marched inside, looked around at the full room, and said, "Non-mafia, out!"

Ninety-five percent of the bar emptied, including the bartender.

The four men who'd come in started to move towards Stephan, but my boys handled them easily, knocking them all out and dropping them unceremoniously to the floor before zip-tying their hands and feet together.

Stephan continued his uninterrupted walk to the cage and glared inside. "Explain."

"This crazy bitch attacked us," the boss said and clutched his bleeding shoulder. "I demand retribution."

"You come into my territory, threaten me, then infiltrate again and hit one of my family and think *you'll* get retribution?" Stephan asked. His scowl turned into a smile as he exploded in a fit of laughter. "You're dumber than Connor let on!"

"Excuse me?" the man demanded but stumbled a step.

"You okay, Amelia?" Stephan asked me.

I walked closer to the cage exit with my eyes focused on the average boss. "Yes, sir. Awaiting orders."

"See, the thing is that I can only control my people to a

certain degree," Stephan said. "Not only did you piss *her* off when you hit her, but you pissed off all of her lovers as well. The four of them see that red welt swelling on her face and your death is the only thing on their minds right now. I'm afraid even if I order them to let you go, that they'll just inter-pret my order as 'let you go for tonight' and tomorrow, you'll have one or more of them standing over your bed right before they put a bullet in your brain or a knife through your heart. You hurt their treasure, also one of my treasures, and that cannot go unpunished. So, it leaves me in a very salty pickle. Do I order them to leave you alone, knowing they'll find some way to bypass my order? Or, do I kill you right here and now for infiltrating my territory, hurting my family, and thinking you are more than you are?"

"I'll leave," the man pleaded. "I'll leave and never enter your territory again."

"Not good enough," Shea snarled. Was it possible that he looked bigger than usual? He totally looked bigger than usual.

"See?" Stephan said and shrugged. "You know what? You are all adults. Amelia, why don't you come with me to the car and we'll let these gentlemen figure things out between themselves?"

"I didn't finish my drink," I protested for some reason.

"Bring it with us," he said and dipped his chin to give me a look.

As I glanced around at my men, I understood. There was a lot of hostility in all of their eyes and I needed to leave before my presence escalated things further.

I grabbed my drink, handed Arcadio the dagger I had pulled from the dude's shoulder, and walked outside with Stephan.

"I swear, I was behaving!"

Stephan laughed and opened the door to the SUV. "I never said anything to the contrary."

"You were totally thinking that this incident is my fault, and while I may have brought that douche canoe into the cage with us by trying to scam him for money, I did not escalate things. Wait…" I thought back to how the altercation had started and sighed. "Okay, I totally did it, but only after I found out he was the asshat who cut our power and stuff. I'm sorry. I'm going to be punished again, aren't I?"

"Technically, Arcadio was the first to draw blood, so you won't be punished. He will be punished and will have to retake some of his anger management lessons," Stephan answered, but despite the seriousness of everything he was smiling like it was the funniest thing he'd experienced.

"You're not mad?" I asked as I sipped on my drink, sitting in the middle seat, one leg propped up on the other middle seat, and my back leaned against the door behind me.

Stephan was turned from the front seat so he could look at me. "No, I'm not mad. We were actually trying to find him because there had been rumors that he was in our territory and it was pissing me off."

"Well, I guess I'm glad I could be of service then!" I said in a chipper tone and raised my glass to him. "Cheers."

"So, how was your date up until this event?" he asked.

"Actually, it was really nice. I've never been to a bar like this and was having a lot of fun. We'd made a bet, but didn't get a chance to finish our games before those guys showed up and started talking shit."

"Would you like me to build an ax-throwing cage at our new place?" Stephan asked.

My mouth dropped. "Serious?"

He chuckled, reached back, and set his hand on my knee.

"Darling, I'll build you whatever you want at our new place. Name it and it'll be done."

"Full boxing ring!" I shouted and then covered my mouth with one hand. "Sorry for yelling."

He smiled and nodded. "Done. What else?"

"I get to make a list?" I asked, my eyes wide.

"I want to hear you tell me what you would want in your ideal house if money were not an issue. I don't want you to just give me a list, but tell me all the things so I can see from your expression which things you truly want," he said.

He didn't need to twist my arm. I could list a ton of things that I wanted in my dream home. I'd thought about it enough over the years. "A theater, a spa that's big enough for us all to sit in, a jetted tub in my bedroom or at least a nearby bathroom, a bowling alley, a full bar that's right next to a legitimate dancefloor where I could host a dance party if I wanted to and people would think it was a room in a club, a—"

My desire explosion was interrupted when Arcadio opened the door behind me and I fell out of the SUV.

He caught me with a grunt. "Why are you leaning against the door?"

Somehow, I'd managed to adjust my glass so I didn't spill my drink. "No party foul!"

There was a sigh and several chuckles behind me.

"Time to go home," Arcadio told me, helped me get back into the SUV, and shook his head at me.

"Um, what about the douche canoe average boss guy?" I asked.

"Our cleaning crew is coming," Shea said from the seat behind me.

I tilted my head back to look at him upside down. "Oh, good, you're back to normal size."

He blinked at me. "What?"

"How many drinks did she have?" Forrest asked Arcadio.

"Not that many," he whispered.

"A porch swing!" I yelled.

Everyone looked at me, except Dane who was driving.

"What?" Arcadio asked.

Stephan chuckled. "On the front or back? First floor or off your room?"

"We're missing something," Shea mumbled. "They must have been talking while we were occupied."

"First floor, back of the house. I want to sit in it and look out over our property behind us, where I'd like cherry trees so in the spring, I can see all the pretty blossoms," I answered.

"What about roses?" Stephan asked.

"We're so out of the loop," Dane whispered.

"Honestly, I'm not a huge fan of roses. The thorns hurt."

"You're supposed to look at them, not fall into them," Forrest commented.

I mocked him silently and took a big chug of my drink.

Stephan's phone rang and he answered without looking at the caller ID, a huge smile on his face. "Yes?"

The smile quickly disappeared as he listened to the person on the phone. "You've no idea what transpired. If you'd like to continue this discussion, I'm more than willing to."

I looked at Arcadio who shrugged.

"I think that would be ill-advised, but that decision is up to you," Stephan continued, his serious tone in full effect. "I'll let you sleep on it." He hung up and sighed.

"I'm sorry," I whispered, somehow knowing I messed something up.

"Who was that?" Shea asked.

"The younger brother of the man you just killed. Apparently, he had a monitor on him and his brother was able to see what happened," Stephan explained. "He is claiming he will start a war with us if he is not properly compensated."

"What's he want for proper compensation?" I asked. "A million? Two?"

"You," Stephan answered.

I sighed and shook my head. "Is it really so hard for these guys to get laid?"

There were several snickers covered by coughs in the SUV.

"It's more about taking something we care about since we killed something he cared about," Stephan explained.

"What are you going to do?" I asked. I knew he wasn't going to give me over to them, but that didn't mean I knew what his plan was.

"Look at you, going on a date and almost starting a mafia war. Quite the night, huh?" Shea teased behind me.

I looked at him upside down again and glared. "Ox, I'm a woman of many talents. Starting shit has always been one of them."

"Gorgeous, we knew that the moment we saw you in that coffee shop," Forrest purred behind me.

I turned my head to look at him, fake tears pooling in my eyes as I pouted. "Am I such a bad person?"

His eyes widened. "N-no, I was just teasing, I—"

Leaning forward, as far as the seatbelt would let me, I exploded into a fit of laughter. "Your face!" More laughter rendered me unable to speak.

"I swear, she didn't drink that much," Arcadio shouted.

I looked over at Arcadio and saw that Shea was glaring and seemed ready to kill him.

"Oh!" I shouted.

Everyone looked at me, even Dane in the rearview mirror.

"A secret bar in my bedroom that I can hit a button on the wall or something and this cute little cabinet of alcohol comes out of," I said.

Stephan smirked. "I think we should have that in every room."

"Yes!" I yelled. "Please. Oh, my gosh. Please do that; that would be the best thing ever. I will even put me in charge of keeping it stocked. Can you imagine inviting someone over, hitting a button, or light fixture, and then a fully stocked bar slides out? That would be rich-person epic! That's like… Batman-level epic."

"What is going on?" Arcadio asked.

"She's giving me her wish list," Stephan explained.

"Can we have secret passageways? Oh, that probably won't work since the house is already built, huh? Crap. I've always wanted secret passageways. So I could, like, sneak from my room to Stephan's without the guests knowing or to escape if invaders came and wanted to kill us. Can't kill me if I'm in the walls!"

"Secret passageways could be added on, but they'd decrease the size of the rooms because new walls would have to be added," Stephan said.

"I mean, do we really need huge rooms, anyway?" I asked.

"I do," Dane protested.

"Okay, so no secret passages to Dane's room then," I said with a wide smile. "Problem solved."

Everyone laughed, and despite our situation, it was a great way to end the night.

CHAPTER NINE

After checking my luggage for the thirtieth time, panicking for the third time, taking a flight to London, a plane to Dubai, staying the night there, and then a luxurious limo ride, we finally made it onto the cruise ship.

"Holy icebergs! This thing is humongous!" I gasped.

"That's what she said!" Dane and Arcadio yelled.

That earned us several disapproving looks from the old couples boarding the ship with us. The women all wore huge diamond rings that had to weigh a ton.

"I get that they want to show off how expensive their rings are, but doesn't that give them carpal tunnel lugging those diamonds around?" I muttered to myself.

"Someone's jealous," Forrest whispered in my ear.

I looked up at him. "Am not. I don't want to scratch myself every time I try to wipe my butt."

He snorted a laugh. "I never expect what comes out of your mouth."

"Let's get inside, get through the safety briefings, and then we can find our rooms," Stephan said and gently pushed my lower back. He'd somehow gotten the other mafia to not start a war with us, which I was very grateful for, but I knew it had cost him monetarily. Somehow, I would make it up to him, I just wasn't sure how.

The safety briefings were boring and terrifying at the same time. I definitely did not want a reenactment of the *Titanic*.

Stephan escorted me to my room, ordering the others to go find their rooms, and then we'd meet up for dinner.

My room was actually connected to his, much larger than I expected with a window that let me see the ocean we sailed through, had a king-sized bed, and a balcony with a jacuzzi we shared. The bed was incredibly soft just from the brief seat I'd taken to remove my shoes and set my bag down.

"This had to have cost you a lot," I said as I entered the shared living room where Stephan stood.

He smirked. "It was worth every penny to see your expression just now."

I spun around and narrowed my eyes. "Is that why you sent the others away?"

He chuckled. "You know me so well."

"Thank you, again, for doing this."

He smiled. "You're welcome. Now, I'm going to go into my room and unpack. We'll meet for dinner, okay?"

I nodded and returned his smile. "Sounds good."

Once he was gone, I tossed my suitcase on the bed and started unpacking into the walk-in closet. Who knew I could have a walk-in closet on a cruise ship?

I also had my own bathroom, a sauna, a massage table for when I wanted a private massage, and decorations that looked like they were worth thousands. After putting on a cute dress, touching up my makeup, and doing a few twirls in the floor to ceiling mirrors, I headed down to the dining room.

"Boo!" Shea said behind me.

I gasped and spun around, hand reaching towards my hidden dagger.

His eyes caught the movement and he smirked. "Oh, I am so prepared for you to stab me."

I choked on my cough. "That's what she said."

He pulled me forward and kissed me, his enormous frame wrapped around mine and made the moment feel completely intimate and private even though I knew there were people walking by us.

When he pulled back, my face was flushed and I panted.

"Ready for dinner?" he asked with a smirk.

"Smug jerk," I whispered as I spun out of his hold and walked into the room.

With his large frame behind me, I walked in with my head held high and zero fear.

"Where?" I asked over my shoulder without looking back. I was too short to see around most of the tall men standing around, but I knew my giant would be able to spot our group easily.

"Nine o'clock," Shea answered behind me.

I turned in that direction, scanning the tables where people were already seated, spotted our group, and headed that way.

When I approached, Dane, Forrest, and Stephan stood.

"Oh, we're being such gentlemen on this trip," I commented. "Perhaps I should have worn a tiara."

Shea pushed in my seat as I sat and whispered in my ear, "I'll buy you whatever type of tiara or crown you want so long as you wear it while you ride me."

I had started to drink out of my water cup, but his statement had me coughing and spluttering.

People began to look in our direction.

Quickly, I put my napkin over my mouth and coughed into it. "Dammit, Ox."

He sat across from me, his proud smile bright and warm in the dim lighting of the ballroom.

"What do you want to drink?" Dane asked.

I shrugged. "Something yummy."

He nodded, stood, and walked to a side wall where a bartending station was.

"What do you think so far?" Forrest asked.

"It's really big and a bit confusing to navigate," I admitted. "I am *very* excited for the ball."

"Looking forward to dancing with us?" Shea asked.

"Among other things," I said and tried, but failed, to hide my smirk.

"So, we wanted to ask how you preferred to spend the days here," Stephan said. "We can either split our time with you individually or spend it all together as a group."

My brows furrowed. "I thought the plan was to get alone time together?"

"We can do that for sure," he said and nodded. "We just wanted to offer another option to you in case you weren't up for that."

"I'd love to have more time with each of you individually. I get a lot of time with you all as a group, which I love, but it's so rare that I can spend time one on one. I almost feel bad even asking." The last sentence was said in a whisper as I dropped my head and looked at my hands in my lap.

"It's perfectly normal for you to feel that way," Forrest said and reached over to grip my hand with his. "We know that you don't have a favorite and that you enjoy your time with us in group settings. Honestly, we've all been wanting more alone time with you."

"Great!" I said cheerily. "But don't expect me to put out. A lady has standards."

All of them laughed and shook their heads.

Dane returned and set a bright pink and blue drink in front of me. He took his seat and sipped from his whiskey and water.

With a big gulp, I swallowed the drink and moaned. "Yes."

"What's that drink called?" Forrest asked.

"Panty Dropper," Dane said, cleared his throat, and adjusted his pants in his seat.

A smirk spread as the fire warmed through me. "Oh, that might be an appropriate name."

"Did you look through the pamphlet?" Stephan asked, distracting me and the others.

I nodded. "Yes."

"Are there any events you'd like to participate in?" he asked.

"I'm curious about the submarine excursion," I commented. "It's not something I've ever done before."

Stephan nodded. "We can definitely do that."

"Anything else?" Arcadio asked.

"I'd have to pull out the pamphlet again," I said. "I did mark a few things that seemed interesting, but was a little too distracted staring out the plane's window on the way here to really focus." As much as I hated to admit it, I hadn't traveled too much in my life and all the things I saw from the plane were so pretty and abnormal from my normal life.

"After this, why don't we meet in Stephan's room and discuss the options to plan our time here?" Shea suggested.

Everyone nodded their agreement.

I scoffed and took another drink from my brightly colored alcoholic beverage. "You think I'll be sober enough for that?"

Shea smiled. "Kitten, we just need your highlighted and marked pamphlet. Otherwise, you can just sit in one of our laps and sleep while we work it out."

I set my drink down a bit too hard, crossed my arms, and narrowed my eyes. "I am offended."

His eyes widened a bit.

"He just meant that we can figure out what you'd like to do based on your notes," Arcadio said softly. "We've been talking to you about things you'd like to do for a few weeks now. We should, hopefully, know what you'd like."

"You'd know more if you stubborn asses would make your bucket lists for me," I muttered, picked my drink up, and took a small sip. If I didn't watch it, I'd be drunk before our meal arrived. Not that that was an awful thing, but I wanted to remember my time here.

Looking around, I took in the expensive centerpieces, crystal vases with rare flowers, the beautiful chandeliers, and the shiny silverware that had to be actual silver.

"How much did these tickets cost?" I asked as I inspected my fork.

"You don't need to worry about that," Stephan said. "You just need to enjoy yourself and have as much fun as you can possibly have."

That meant they cost way more than I could even imagine.

"Please tell me you didn't spend more than six figures per ticket," I whispered, feeling a little faint at the mere thought of him paying that for one ticket, let alone six tickets.

"We definitely need to get sushi once we're out on the open seas," Dane said, interrupting my question. "I've been dying for some fresh sushi."

"Oh, I haven't had sushi in a few months," I realized. "I definitely need some sushi."

"You also need another drink," Shea said and stood. "Anyone else need a refill?"

Everyone raised their hands, which made Shea chuckle before he headed off to the bar. He could have easily just summoned a waiter to our table, but I knew the guys liked to do things like this, more like an average person.

"You're smirking," Arcadio commented.

"I enjoy that you guys try to do things like getting your own drinks, despite the fact that we have a butler assigned to our rooms," I said.

"It helps us stay humble," Forrest explained. "We don't want to forget our roots, where we came from, and get used to the 'high life.'"

"You don't realize how far you've ascended," I shook my head sadly.

Arcadio reached over and gripped my hand. "We know, Sweets."

"That's part of why we wanted to bring you on a trip like this. We wanted you to experience true luxury. More so than what you experience in our home," Stephan said with a soft smile.

My drink was empty, so I looked through the glass at him like it was a spyglass. "You're buttering me up for something."

He chuckled. "What makes you think that?"

"I know you," I said, and set my glass down, a little too forcefully. "What is it? Is there bad news you're going to deliver?"

He scowled and then his brows smoothed as his expression softened. "No, darling. There is no bad news. Just fun to be had."

I didn't buy it, but pushing the issue would only cause discourse and this was supposed to be a fun trip. So, for now, I would let it lie.

…For now…

"How is it going with the mansion purchase?" I asked.

Stephan looked at Forrest.

"Our offer has been accepted and by the time we return, we should be through the escrow period and ready to start your improvements before moving in," he answered with a smile.

"We need to figure out rooms," I said and tapped a finger on the table. "And layout for the other rooms. I'll need all of that done before I can determine where to put the artillery."

"Did she just say artillery?" Shea asked as he returned with a tray of drinks.

"You know we paid good money for the waiters to do that for us," Stephan commented.

Shea set the tray down, keeping the drinks perfectly balanced the whole time, and then put my drink in front of me. "Yes, but then I wouldn't be able to impress Amelia like this."

"How'd you know I was impressed?" I asked. I was, but I hadn't said anything. Had I?

He kissed my cheek. "Your eyes give you away every time, Kitten."

At some point, he had rolled back the sleeves of his long-sleeved button-up shirt, so I watched as his forearms flexed, his veins bulged, and my panties got wet while he distributed drinks.

"You okay?" Arcadio asked me.

I cleared my throat and took a drink instead of answering. Definitely okay.

An older man in a tuxedo stood on a stage I hadn't noticed until the spotlight shone on it. "Thank you for joining us on this adventure. The first course is served."

On cue, dozens of servers in tuxedos glided into the room carrying silver trays and began distributing salads.

The man continued talking, droning on about how excited he was and some other crap, but my ravenous stomach had forced my eyes to focus on the salad as it was brought to our table and set before me. Mixed greens, dried cranberries, and a dressing that made me salivate even more adorned the salad. I hadn't realized how unladylike my eating was until a woman at a nearby table began to fan herself.

I looked up at my men and smiled apologetically.

"You should have told me you were so hungry," Stephan chastised. "We could have had a snack brought up to our room."

"We barely boarded," I reminded him. "Honestly, I didn't realize how hungry I was until just now."

"It doesn't matter if we were just walking onto the ship," Forrest said. "If you wanted something to eat, we could have ordered things sent to the room ahead of us. Just remember that for next time, okay?"

"You're all acting worried, but it's really okay," I said with a chuckle. "I've gone days without eating before. I'm just too spoiled now."

The words left my mouth and I immediately wished to take them back as all of their faces dropped and fire filled their eyes.

"I don't want you to ever go hungry again," Arcadio said softly and reached over to grab my hand.

I squeezed his hand and smiled. "It's been over a decade

since anything like that has happened. Deep breath, guys. Big, deep, cleansing breaths."

They all obeyed and I almost squealed in delight when steak and steamed broccoli was brought out for our next course.

"Don't make yourself sick," Dane commented as I began cutting into my steak.

"Right," I agreed with a nod. "Best to pace myself. I don't want to miss out on dessert."

"She's going to give herself the itis," Forrest said with a smirk.

I pouted. "Don't jinx me!"

"You do this to yourself all the time," Arcadio said and shook his head. "You eat fast and too much and then get sleepy, aka the itis."

The itis was the worst. After big meals, especially ones with lots of carbs, I'd get super sleepy and need to rest for at least half an hour before I could do anything.

"So, what's on the agenda for tonight?" I asked, slowing my eating down and being sure I thoroughly chewed my steak before swallowing. You didn't realize how little you chewed food when you were hungry until a piece got stuck. I never wanted that to happen again.

"Dancing and then whatever you want," Stephan answered.

"So, tonight isn't one of your nights?" I asked and looked at all of them.

They all shook their heads.

"Tonight is your night," Stephan replied with a smirk.

"So, we could dance a bit and then I could relax in the hot tub with a drink by myself?"

That question earned me some frowns from Dane and Arcadio, but Stephan just continued to smirk and nodded.

Focusing on my food again, I didn't speak for several minutes, instead letting the guys whisper amongst themselves.

"So, tomorrow will be my day," Stephan informed me.

Somehow, I managed not to spit out my drink in shock. Like a pro, I dabbed at my lips before asking, "Oh? You're taking the first day?"

He smiled. "We drew straws and I was lucky enough to be first."

"Rigged," Shea coughed into his hand and smiled.

"Do you have plans for us?" I asked softly. Tomorrow night was the ball, which was when I'd wear my fancy dress.

His face resumed its usual neutral, almost bored, expression. "One or two things."

"Well, I guess I better make sure not to drink more than this second drink so I'm not hungover and unable to appreciate your plans," I said. Despite the statement, I still chugged the rest of my drink.

You couldn't waste good booze!

"You enjoy yourself as much as you want," Stephan said. "We will adjust our plans around your abilities."

For some reason, I felt insulted, but shrugged it off, smiled, and said, "Then I'll have another!"

CHAPTER TEN

I should not have had another or the two more that followed that. My hangover was one to be recorded as an example of what not to do.

After my drinking adventures I'd slept most of the day away and now the sun was well on its way to setting. Hunched over the toilet, I dry heaved for the twentieth time.

"I'm so sorry," I apologized for the dozenth time to Stephan who refused to leave me alone.

He stroked my hair. "You don't need to apologize to me. There are enough days on this trip that I can have my day with you tomorrow instead. Focus on getting better."

After brushing my teeth, I walked to my bed, Stephan's arm around me to assist, and laid down.

"You need to hydrate," Stephan said sternly. "If you can't get this drink down, I'll have the doctor insert an IV."

Having IVs hurt and I despised them. "I'm trying to keep it down," I whined. "It's not my fault that I can't keep it in my stomach."

"I'm going to call the doctor. You lay there and rest," he ordered me.

As he walked out of my room, he left the door open, and a small smile lifted my lips despite feeling awful. The others had taken care of me before when I'd been sick, but this was the first time that Stephan was with me.

He returned with a tray of toast, electrolyte drinks, and plain water. "Eat and drink something, please."

After sitting up, I took a piece of the buttered toast and nibbled on the edge. "You can send one of the others in if you want." Despite saying it, I really hoped he would stay.

Brows furrowed, he asked, "Am I doing this wrong? I admit that I haven't taken care of someone with a hangover in a very long time, but I thought I was doing alright."

"You're doing great!" I blurted. "I just meant that I'm sure you have important things to attend to and you don't want to spend the day babysitting my stupid ass."

He sat on the edge of my bed and gently took my free hand. "I want to stay with you, and help you get better, but I won't be offended if you'd rather have one of the others."

I shook my head vehemently but then had to exhale harshly to stop the dizziness. "No, please. I'm sorry. I want you to stay. I...like having you with me. It's been so long since you and I had some alone time together." I honestly could not remember the last time we'd been alone. It was a very rare occurrence.

"I know and I'm sorry. I need to make more time for you. Connor actually chastised me the last time we spoke. Apparently Erina was very upset to hear that you and I rarely had time together and he was certain to instill in me the importance of spending time with you. I know he's right; it was a good reminder that even though I am the CEO of my company, the Boss of our mafia, and an overall busy man, I still need to make sure that you're taken care of. With the others, I thought you wouldn't need or want me around much, but it's clear that's not the case. I will do better. I promise."

Stunned into silence, I nibbled more on my toast and drank some of the flavored electrolyte water.

"I'm sorry that they brought up our relationship," I whispered after a moment. "I should stop talking so openly to Erina about things."

He chuckled and shook his head. "It's a good thing that you have a friend like her. It's rare for women involved in the mafia to have another person they can relate to. Honestly, having Connor as an ally is a huge advancement for us and I have you to thank for that."

"Well, me and my notoriously nosey self" I chuckled.

"Inquisitive is what I would call you," he corrected with his own chuckle.

"Did he tell you about their upcoming celebration?" I asked. I hadn't mentioned it to the others because they'd already freaked out about me going over for a single night.

He nodded. "Yes, and now that we are allies, it will be easier to clear. You'll take at least two of your guards with you."

"Two? That will leave you more vulnerable."

"We have others who can guard me," he said with a soft smile.

I shook my head. "No, it's too important a week for you to not have your most trusted guards."

The same week that Erina was having a huge anniversary celebration, Stephan was releasing a new drone to the public.

He would be attending several conferences and would need his best guards at his side to keep him safe.

"What do you propose?" he asked and folded his hands in his lap.

"Erina and Marlee will both be with me. We will be at Connor's casino, which will be *heavily* guarded, Marlee will have her guard, and Erina will likely have at least one of her husbands with her. I can go without the guys to allow you to be more protected since my friends will afford me protection just by being with them. I will promise to stay out of trouble, stay in the casino's walls, and allow you to drop me off and pick me up if it would make you feel better."

His head tilted slightly as he contemplated my suggestion. "I'll agree to those terms if you agree to mine."

Waiting patiently was never my strong suit, but when it came to Stephan, I knew it was best to hold my tongue.

"After the event, I will assign you a bodyguard. This person will be your shadow in all future outings, even going to Erina's. You can order him to stay out of the room, but he will be within a few seconds of you at all times, even at our mansion. His sole purpose will be to throw himself between you and a bullet, or carry you away from a dangerous situation."

My brows rose into my hairline. "Why the sudden desire to protect me in that way? You know I'm capable of protecting myself, handling weapons, and generally staying out of trouble. What happened that you aren't telling me?"

He shook his head and smiled sadly. "You truly don't understand how I feel about you. I suppose that is my fault. Being asexual makes it a bit harder to show modern women how you feel about them since I'm not as affectionate as the others."

My throat suddenly felt dry and it was difficult to swallow. Was he telling me that he…loved me? Romantically?

"Is she okay?" Shea asked, bursting into the room and interrupting our moment.

Dane was right behind him, rushing over to immediately put his hand against my forehead.

I swatted his hand away. "I'm fine. Just hungover. What got you two all in a tizzy?"

Stephan stood, smoothed down his slacks, and said, "You two are as impetuous as ever. Out. Go on. She's fine."

Dane scowled, kissed my cheek, and left the room.

"The ball was rescheduled to tomorrow night," Shea informed me, squatted down so we were eye level, and kissed the tip of my nose. "There's supposed to be a storm tonight, so if you get scared, come to our room, okay?"

"Will the ship capsize?" I asked, breathless not from fear, but from the weight of the affection of these wonderful men.

"No, the storm won't be that strong," Stephan answered before Shea could. "It's just a precaution to ensure no one's glass tips over or loses their balance while dancing drunk."

That had me breathing a little easier. "Good."

"Go on, Ox," Stephan ordered Shea. "Out."

Shea gave me a small pout, which made me smile, kissed my cheek, and left.

Once they were gone, Stephan shook his head and chuckled. "I underestimated their level of worry surrounding you."

At some point, I'd finished the toast and was feeling better. "Can we go on a walk around the ship?" I asked and stood. "I'll bring my electrolyte water with me and drink it as we go."

Stephan looked at me a moment and then nodded. "The sunlight would be good for you. Get changed and I'll show you around the ship and let you see all the luxuries that are available while we're here."

Changing took longer than I anticipated, but once I was done, and took a two-minute rest, Stephan and I left the room.

"How many of these have you gone on?" I asked curiously as he walked at my side, his hands clasped behind his back.

"This is my fourth time on a cruise," he answered.

"You know, I realized that I don't really know much about your past, from your point of view." The words came out quietly, a realization more than a request for information.

He stopped a moment before resuming our casual pace, no doubt this slow because of my dehydration. "I suppose that's true. Would you like me just to sum up my life?"

"How about we trade stories," I said with a wide smile. "You tell me a story from your past and I'll tell you one of mine. It'll be a bonding experience and you can tell me whatever stories you want, which will prevent me from prying."

Stephan laughed quietly as he looked over at me. "I doubt anyone could prevent you from prying when you're set on learning something."

"I will take that as a compliment," I said, my smile widening even more.

He looked back in front of us, his movements almost automatic-looking as he moved in front of me when someone else approached from the opposite direction of the hallway and then resuming his place at my side after they passed. We turned left, exited a door that led to the very side of the ship, giving us a balcony we could look out over the water from. Instead of stopping, he continued walking, headed towards the front of the ship.

"My parents died when I was a toddler, and I was adopted

by my only surviving family member: my father's brother. He was a shrewd man, spoke very little, hated loud noises, and had never wanted children. However, he loved my father like a best friend and with me looking exactly like him, minus my mother's eyes, he couldn't turn me away. I don't remember the first few years of life with him, but he assured me that they were frustrating. It took him many years to find a way to occupy my brain so that I wasn't running around his mansion like a hellion. Once he introduced me to electronics, I was hooked, and haven't looked back. It's all thanks to him that I created this empire."

"He sounds like a great man," I replied, processing his tale a bit still.

"Your turn," he said, beaming, and kept his gaze on mine as we continued walking.

"I was spoiled as a child, with my mother having multiple partners, I was never wanting when it came to gifts. Attention, though, was something I craved and so I acted out and did what I could to get more of it. One time, I lit a small shed I'd built on fire. They all ran out, anxious to see if I was safe, and since we couldn't put it out, we stood together and watched it burn. That was when I realized that I definitely needed therapy."

He was quiet for several moments before saying, "That explains a lot about you."

My eyes narrowed as I glared at him. "Excuse me?"

Smirking, he said, "Not in a bad way. I just mean that being raised with a polyamorous mother and seeking attention explains why you'd willingly enter into an arrangement like the one we have."

"It seems like I should be offended, but I'm not," I said, and shrugged one shoulder.

His laughter echoed around us like a warm breeze on a cool night.

"Your turn," I reminded him, and put my hands behind my back as we continued walking, coming out to a pool area with lounge chairs filled with older women with their ginormous rings.

Being with multiple men meant I likely wouldn't get a ring, which made me sad, but since my runner's up prize was several hot men, I was okay with it.

After a night of exchanging childhood experiences, I felt a lot closer to Stephan. Although he'd been aloof often, he was a warm and welcoming man, and I enjoyed being so close to him.

The next day we swam, ate snacks poolside, and drank delicious beach-themed concoctions until it was time to prepare for dinner.

This dinner was the one I was going to make my appearance at. The one I was going to wear was the gorgeous dress Erina had purchased for me.

If only I had a team to do my hair and makeup for me!

With no other option, I went to work on my own hair and makeup.

Thankfully, Erina, Marlee, and I had gone over makeup ideas, and I'd saved several pictures and tutorials so I could do an okay job without help.

By the time I finished my makeup, I barely had time to curl my hair and get dressed.

The dress was tight and I almost had to call out for assistance, but thankfully I managed it on my own. Erina's dressmaker had outdone herself. The dress had one shoulder, hugged my frame, had a triangle of lace that went from my belly button around to expose the left side of my stomach and tapered towards the middle of my back. There were delicate folds that added to the shape and a slit up the right leg to my upper thigh, just high enough to be sexy and not too much. It was a deep olive color and looked great with my skin tone.

Stephan had gone to Forrest's room to discuss something with him, leaving me free to use the suite as needed and have full privacy.

Ready, appearance triple checked, and a shot to settle my nerves, I headed down to the ballroom.

Just outside stood Stephan in a dark suit with a white shirt that was opened instead of with a tie like he'd normally wear. It made his sexual allure ten times stronger and I sucked in a sharp breath as I took him in.

The breath drew his attention and as he looked over at me, his eyes widened and he took two large steps towards me. "Amelia, you look…phenomenal. I thought the dress you'd worn to the gala was the epitome of allure, but this…This dress was created to be worn by you. Everyone who sees you tonight is being given a gift they have no hope of deserving. Aphrodite would pale in comparison to you tonight."

My cheeks warmed. "You always have such a way with words, Stephan. I can understand why so many women are after you. If you weren't asexual, I'd be asking you up to my room instead of going into this ball." After that awkward admission, I dropped my head to look at the floor between us.

"Darling," he whispered and gently tilted my chin up with his finger. "I'm asexual, but not aromantic. I thought I was for a bit, but I found myself drawn to you in ways I wasn't with other women. I know that I cannot fulfill your sexual needs but the others can. I had hoped I'd made my feelings clear, but obviously, I need to be more forward and I will rectify that this evening."

"How would a relationship like this work, exactly?" I asked softly. "I care a lot about you, Stephan, and am likely already in too deep anyway, but I'd like to make sure I don't overstep any boundaries or make you upset by trying to do something you don't want to."

"I enjoy hand-holding, light touches, cuddling, and pets, as you know. I just don't enjoy things beyond that. I'm even good with cheek kisses and long hugs. I would like to continue to develop a romantic relationship with you that involves most of the perks, minus the sex."

"What if it doesn't work out?" I asked, feeling like a nervous teenager all over again. "What if you decide that you can't or don't want to continue a romantic relationship with me?"

He leaned forward and rubbed his nose against mine. "You have already claimed a spot in my heart as a friend. I doubt anything will change that. Besides, my men love you and I wouldn't dare cause issues there."

"So, if I wanted to hold your hand while we go out into the ballroom, in public, in front of all of those people—not just as a social requirement but because I wanted to..." I let the question linger since he knew what I was getting at.

Immediately, he reached down and grabbed my hand, lacing our fingers together. "Let's go."

With no further preamble, he pushed open the doors and walked into the ballroom with his fingers laced between mine, his head held high, and a wide smile on his face.

When we approached our table, Arcadio, Shea, Dane, and Forrest stood, their eyes wide and a few slack-jawed.

Stephan cleared his throat and they all met my eyes.

"I hadn't realized a goddess could descend to grace us with her presence," Forrest said as he bent and kissed the back of my free hand.

Shea, Arcadio, and Dane bowed repeatedly while chanting, "We are not worthy!"

Laughter burst from me and I had to quickly look up at the fancy chandelier nearby to keep from tearing up. "I love you all."

"Care to dance?" Stephan asked.

I turned and lifted one side of my dress and gave a half curtsy. "It would be my honor, sir."

Stephan immediately spun me out onto the dancefloor, his grip somehow both loose and tight at the same time, giving me the semblance of safety despite it just being a single hand.

The band played a more upbeat song and Stephan led me into a waltz I had not been prepared for but was pleasantly surprised with.

"Did your uncle force you to take dancing lessons?" I asked as we swirled around the older couples.

His smile was infectious and after only a few turns my own smile matched his. "Yes," he answered after a moment. "It was imperative to him that I learn to dance."

"Well, I wish I could thank him," I said as he continued to spin us around, gaining a lot of attention from the other attendees.

"We also learned," Shea said as he spun into us, stole my hands, and took me from Stephan's hold.

Stephan's chuckle was all I heard as we merged back with the other dancers.

"Why, Ox, it almost seems like you might be...jealous," I said with a smirk.

His huge frame blocked out the others around us and made it feel like we were dancing alone. "I've not been able to touch you for an entire twenty-four-hour period. It's been absolute torture."

I gave him a big-lipped pout. "I would never want to torture you."

"You, in that dress, is the most torturous thing I've ever endured," he whispered as he leaned closer. "I want to slide it up your body and worship you in front of everyone here."

Yes, please.

"Well, I appreciate the offer," I said much too breathlessly. "Perhaps in the morning, you can show me exactly what you meant."

His tongue darted out to lick my neck. "It's a date."

A small gasp escaped before I could stop it, but the next second Shea had handed me off to Forrest.

"For being the first one to spot you, I've barely gotten even a glimpse of you these past few weeks, little goddess," he commented as we slowed to match the speed of the slow dance playing.

"Don't blame me," I said and shrugged. "You've been busy with preparing for the upcoming events. I've sashayed past your desk in short dresses several times trying to get your attention."

"Oh, you've gotten my attention, but I haven't been able to do more than salivate and nurse blue balls," he said loud enough that a few nearby women gasped and turned away from us.

"Yet, aside from a few quick encounters, my bed has been incredibly empty," I commented and arched a brow.

He shrugged. "Those *quick* encounters were all I could

manage with my schedule. From the way you screamed my name, it didn't seem like they were too quick, though."

A huge smile split my face. "Definitely not." In truth, they'd been far more attentive to my sexual needs the past month than the previous months and while I often slept alone, my needs were definitely met.

"We know that we need to do more and neglect you less. We don't deserve you," he whispered.

"I'm extremely spoiled and anyone would kill to be in my situation," I said as we continued to dance.

"You deserve the stars, but I am too short to reach them," Dane said as he tugged me out of Forrest's hold and into his arms.

"Did you all plan your best pickup lines for tonight?" I asked as I placed my hands on his chest to steady myself.

"Pretty sure whatever thoughts we had were obliterated the moment we saw you in this dress with that makeup," he said as he stared into my eyes. "You truly look magnificent, Amelia."

I smirked. "So, you're saying that if I walked by right now you would totally ditch the guys to come hit on me?"

He nodded emphatically. "One thousand percent."

Why did that one statement hike my self-confidence up so much?

Before we could talk more, Arcadio stole me from Dane and spun me. "Hello, Aphrodite. Were the peasants bothering you? Should I smite them for you?"

I tapped my chin as he spun us around the dancefloor. "That is an interesting proposition, but perhaps we can put a pin in that for now?"

He smiled. "As you wish."

Leaning forward, I kissed his cheek. "So, when do we get our day?"

"In two days," he answered and rubbed his cheek against mine. "I'll be counting the hours until I get you alone."

"There's a dark corner not too far away that I'm sure we could disappear into for a few minutes," I commented, mostly joking...sort of joking...kind of joking.

He choked as he laughed and had to stop dancing to cough. "Dammit, Amelia."

Stephan took that moment to take my hand, pull me to the middle of the dancefloor, and then, stopped. The spotlights shone upon him as he dropped to one knee and held up an opened ring box towards me. "Amelia, you tumbled into my life, nestled into my heart, and have taken up residence. Every time I look to the future, my visions surround you. There's no life for me without you at my side. Will you marry me?"

The diamond ring in the box rivaled any of the ones I had seen. My hands flew to my mouth and I gaped at him.

Was this real?

Was I hallucinating?

Had Stephan Moriarty really just asked me to marry him?

I glanced at Arcadio and the others who were lined up nearby and it was clear this wasn't just me marrying Stephan, but me marrying all of them. Much like Erina had done with Connor.

I nodded, a huge smile splitting my face. "Yes. Yes, I will marry you."

Several people clapped, but I paid them little mind as Stephan slipped the ring onto my finger, stood, and kissed my cheek. "I love you, Amelia."

I threw my arms around his neck. "I love you, too, Stephan."

The others approached and I hugged and kissed each of them as well, not caring about the strange looks we received as I kissed the others.

"Dinner will be served shortly," a deep voice announced over the PA system.

Stephan took my hand and led me to a table where we all sat down.

I stared at the ring, patted my dress, and scowled. "Crap."

"What?" Dane asked from my left side.

I looked at him. "I need to send a picture to Erina and Marlee! They'll kill me if someone leaks this first."

Stephan held out his phone. "You can text them from mine. Connor and Brian will both know to send it to their wives."

I did as he said, sending to Brian and Connor instead of Marlee and Erina, and immediately received a video call.

Erina appeared on the video with Marlee at her side, both obviously at the pool at her mansion. "Shut up!" Erina shouted at me.

I turned the video around to show her my ring and then turned back to me with a wide smile.

The three of us squealed a moment and then Marlee said, "It's about time!"

"When's the wedding?" Erina asked.

"Girl, I just accepted," I reminded her with a laugh. "I'm just telling you two before someone leaks it."

Marlee furiously typed on her screen. "Bitch, I'm so ahead of you. I'm leaking this shit first!"

"I told you that dress would work! How long until you come back? We've got to start planning. You should do two weddings like I did: one for the press of you and Stephan and one for you to marry them all. I've still got all my notes and things."

"I'm ordering you a wedding planner right now," Marlee said, still typing on her screen.

"Did you make that dress app yet?" Erina asked. "It would be super helpful to determine what kind of wedding dress you want. Do you know what style of dress you want? Please tell me you aren't going full white, that's so boring."

"I love you two bitches, but I'm hanging up now," I informed them with a laugh and shook my head. "I'll call you when I'm home."

"Love you!" they both yelled before I hit the "end" button.

"They're incorrigible," Stephan said and shook his head as he accepted his phone back.

"Which is a huge part of their charm," I said with a wide smile and continued to look at the incredibly shiny rock on my finger.

"We were worried you might say no," Shea admitted.

My head snapped up to look at him. "What? Why would I say no?"

"If you didn't realize we meant it for you to marry all of us," he said softly, so no one nearby would hear, and trailed off at the end.

"I figured that's what it meant since you were all nearby and didn't look like you wanted to murder Stephan," I chuckled. "Plus, our country doesn't allow for marrying multiple people."

"There are a couple that allow it," Stephan said. "If that's something you want to do."

"Really?" I asked breathlessly. "You'd do that?"

He picked my hand up and kissed my knuckles. "I'd do almost anything for you."

"Champagne to toast in celebration," a waiter said as he set glasses down for us. "Courtesy of the table to your left."

I picked up my glass, turned to the table he indicated, and raised it.

The oldest couple there raised their glasses to us, too.

"That was nice," I said.

Stephan lifted his glass. "To the perfect woman."

"To Amelia!" the guys said.

"To my amazing men," I said. We clinked glasses and drank, then ordered another three rounds before I forced them all out onto the dancefloor with me and paid the DJ to play upbeat songs instead of waltzes.

My heart felt so full that it would explode and I hoped that feeling never went away.

CHAPTER ELEVEN

Shea took me to the theater on the ship and we watched one of my favorite comedies while gorging on popcorn, chocolate, and margaritas.

After we finished the movie, he ordered me to change into a swimsuit.

"What about my ring?" I asked and stared down at the diamond that could blind someone from fifty yards away.

"Look in the ring box," Shea said with a wink and left me with that cryptic message.

I walked into the room and Stephan looked up from his tablet. "Back already?"

"Changing into a swimsuit," I explained, skipped by him, and went to the side table where my ring box sat. After opening it, I realized there was a little tab. I'd thought the box seemed a bit deep for the ring but hadn't investigated it last night.

I'd been three sheets to the wind and only Stephan's strong arm around my waist had allowed me to make it back to our room.

Pulling on the tab in the ring box opened a new compartment where a thin silver band sat.

"Stephan?" I called.

He peeked his head into my room. "Yes?"

"What's this band for? Is it my wedding band?" I stepped to the side so he could see I was looking into the box.

"We figured you'd worry about losing the engagement ring so we got you a band as well."

They really did know me.

My eyes misted and I sniffed. "You're amazing."

He winked. "Don't forget it. You better hurry or Ox will punish you."

I sucked in a breath. "Don't tempt me."

Stephan laughed as he walked away, leaving me to change my outfit and swap out my ring.

They really did think of everything.

Dane waited in the hallway when I exited the room and walked by my side. "You look happy," he commented.

"I am happy," I replied. "Happier than I've ever been in my life."

"It looks good on you," he said and kissed my cheek before resuming walking at my side. "I know it's not my day, but we unanimously decided we didn't want you to walk anywhere alone just in case anyone thinks they're going to use you against Stephan. Now that you've been announced as his fiancée, you're bound to attract even more attention."

I flipped my hair over my shoulder and said, "I've always attracted attention." As soon as I said it, a huge smile split my face and I laughed.

"You're not wrong," he muttered.

"Well, I'd offer to keep a weapon on me, but it's hard to hide a knife or gun in a bikini," I said and indicated my outfit.

His eyes darkened and he said, "Oh, I know."

"So, when is our day?" I asked, my lower body tightening as he continued to stare at me.

"Two more days," he said and shifted his legs as he walked, trying to discreetly adjust his pants to allow for the erection I'd already spotted.

We'd made it to the pool area, so I lifted up on my toes to kiss his cheek. "See you then, Crackers."

He muttered something about a cold shower as he turned away and I enjoyed knowing that my use of his mafia nickname turned him on.

Ox waved at me from the lounge he sat on, a drink menu in his hand.

I smiled and hurried over to him, squeezing to sit on the lounge chair with him instead of the empty one across from his. "What looks good?"

"Oh, I already ordered drinks for us, I was just looking to see if there was something you've not tried that you might like," he explained, as he set the menu down, and looked me over slowly. "Burgundy is a good color on you."

"Thank you for telling me about the other ring," I said and held up my hand to show I had the band on. "You guys are so thoughtful."

He kissed my cheek. "Only for you, Kitten."

"Ox, this isn't a dream, right?" I asked as I leaned my shoulder against his arm. He was so large that my head rested against his shoulder. "I'm not going to wake up tied up in some mafia boss's basement, right?"

His arm wrapped around me and he made a rumbling sound deep in his chest. "That'll never happen again. No one will ever take you from us. I'll burn the fucking world to the ground before I let you fall into harm's way."

Talk about panty-dropping statements.

"Let's get in the water while we wait for our drinks," I said, and headed into the pool that had soft sand at the edge before leading into the twelve-foot-deep pool. It simulated a beach and I honestly couldn't stop myself from curling my toes in the sand a bit as I walked.

"Are there really places with sand this soft?" I asked.

Shea walked just behind me, his huge shadow a welcome darkness at my back. "Yes. We'll have to take you to one on our next vacation."

"You guys don't take vacations often, right?" I asked and glanced over my shoulder, catching him staring at my ass.

"We haven't been, but we will make time to do it more often for you," he said.

"You guys don't need to change your lives for me," I muttered. "I mean, I appreciate it, but I am happy with life as it has been."

His hands came down on my shoulders and he used them to spin me around to face him, the water up to my knees only at this point. "Kitten, we aren't changing our lives in negative ways. We are realizing that we haven't been doing things that we should have, like taking vacations, and that we want to do those things, especially because doing them makes you happy. It's a good thing. You're pointing out things we need to work on. Ways to improve ourselves."

"Did you make your bucket list yet?" I asked, needing to change the subject before I got all weepy.

He nodded, released my shoulders, and walked deeper into the water. "It's only six items, though."

"Only six?" I asked and scowled. "You really only have six things you want to do?"

"Yep. I thought about it for a few weeks, but those are the only items on it."

He knew I was an inquisitive person and was baiting me. Despite wanting to *not* take the bait, I totally did.

"What are they?"

He turned and beamed. "You have to show me yours if I show you mine."

"Mine is over fifty items long," I explained. "It's typed up, but I haven't printed it."

His mouth dropped and brows rose to his hairline. "Fifty?"

I nodded. "I'll tell you four of mine if you'll tell me one of yours."

He stared at me for a long moment, sinking into the water until it was up to his chest, and then nodded. "Deal."

I didn't need to squat for the water to be up to my chest, I actually had to paddle to stay above the water.

While I contemplated what things to tell him, a waiter flagged us down to deliver our drinks. Shea walked out to get them, returning and handing me mine.

I moved closer to the shallow end so I could stand while drinking and talking instead of treading water.

He looked at me expectantly.

"Okay. I want a tiara or crown with real jewels I can wear to events like the gala. I want to go to Scotland and tour castles. I want to visit three countries in one day. I want to have at least one child, but I don't care about the gender."

At my last statement, he spat out part of his drink and started coughing.

"You okay?" I asked with a smirk.

"I just…hadn't expected that last part," he admitted.

"You don't want kids?" I asked and tilted my head to the

side as I drank out of my straw, enjoying the delicious strawberry concoction he had ordered me.

"Oh, I do, very much, but you didn't seem like someone who would want kids," he said after a moment of clearing his throat.

"If I got pregnant, would you want me to have a DNA test, so you could determine who the actual father was?" I asked softly. It wasn't something I'd brought up before, but it was something I probably needed to ask.

He shook his head emphatically. "Definitely not. It doesn't matter which of us is the biological father. All that matters is that it is *your* child and I will love it as my own."

Tears built in my eyes and I quickly blinked them away. "You always know what to say. How does an Ox like you know the right words?"

He chuckled and wrapped an arm around my waist, pulling me against him. "Kitten, I'm not saying what you want to hear. I'm saying what I feel. I will *never* lie to you. Never."

I believed him. In all of my life, I hadn't met another man who was as honest as him. He wanted to protect me, but he wouldn't hide what it was he wanted to protect me from. There were a lot of quote-un-quote *alpha males* who would just try to hide a woman away instead of explaining what the threat was.

"I love you," I whispered. "So much."

He wrapped me up in his arms and kissed me deeply, his tongue tangling with mine in a dance of lust and love. When he pulled back, we were panting. "I love you, too, Amelia. I can't wait to spend the rest of my life with you."

"You have to tell me one of your bucket list items," I reminded him before taking a drink to try to calm my raging heart and hormones.

After a moment he finally answered. "I want to fly a kite."

My mouth dropped. "You've...you've never flown a kite?"

He shook his head. "It wasn't something that was possible during my childhood and seemed ridiculous when I got older, but I would like to do it before I die."

"As soon as we get back, I am taking you kite flying," I said adamantly. "Kites are to be enjoyed and I must show you that enjoyment."

"You can show me whatever you want, kitten."

I didn't miss the innuendo there.

"Wow, didn't take her long to move on," a woman sneered from one of the chairs lining the pool. She wore a gold bikini with chains that draped all the way down her stomach. After drinking from her wine glass, she removed her four diamond bracelets, two sapphire rings, and a sapphire necklace. She carelessly set the jewelry on the table and one of the bracelets immediately started to slip off.

"Hey, your bracelet—"

"Is worth more than you could make if you weren't screwing Stephan Moriarty," she sneered and walked by Shea and me as she swam out into the pool.

"We should get some food," I said, an evil grin spreading on my face.

"I'll go get a menu," Shea said and walked out of the pool.

After admiring the muscles on his back as he walked away, I made my way out, accidentally bumping into the rude woman's table with my hip as I passed. Her bracelet slid to the ground and then beneath the table into a shadow that made it almost impossible to see.

"Whoops," I said softly and finished walking to our chairs.

Shea handed me a menu and I perused my options. "We definitely need chips and salsa as an appetizer," I said.

"How about I order us tacos, too?"

"Great!" I said and handed him back the menu. "You know a girl's favorite three words to hear?"

He smirked. "I love you?"

I shook my head. "I got tacos!"

After placing a kiss on my cheek, he laughed and said, "Well, I better get to ordering them."

"Don't forget the sour cream!" I called after him.

He winked. "Oh, baby, I never forget the cream."

An older woman to our left gasped and put a hand to her chest, which just made me laugh harder.

The towel was super absorbent, the sun warm on my skin, and as I lay on the chair, I closed my eyes. A vacation like this was exactly what I'd wanted. Warm sun, and sexy men. The perfect combination.

"What are you thinking about that has you smirking like that?" Shea asked as he returned.

"I want a tattoo," I said instead of answering him. I opened my eyes just in time to see his widen.

"You do?"

I nodded. "Yep. I want a tattoo."

He sat down on his chair and faced me, his elbows rested on his knees and face in his hands. "What kind of tattoo?" Shea had a lot of tattoos as did the other guys.

"I've been thinking about that for a long time and I think I want a peacock with a bright heart."

His brows rose. "A peacock? Why a peacock?"

"A reminder that I've been surrounded by beautiful men who have offered me grandiose things, but it's the heart that matters the most."

"That's...surprisingly deep."

I put my hands on my hips and glared. "Are you trying to insinuate that I'm not deep?"

"No, it's just that a lot of people get tattoos for random reasons, like it's pretty or I like the colors. I sort of imagined you'd just want a pretty flower or something." He shrugged. "I've got a couple tattoos I had done on a whim. They don't mean anything special and I honestly forget I have them most days."

"Which ones?" I asked and began looking at the tattoos that covered his chest and arms.

"Your food, sir and ma'am," the waiter said as he set a table and the food down between us.

My eyes widened, but then the scent of the food hit my nostrils and I threw a hand over my mouth and nose before running towards the nearest bathroom.

"Amelia!" Shea called after me, but I couldn't respond or I'd throw up all over the pool area.

After emptying my stomach, I washed my face and rinsed out my mouth. Staring at my reflection, I glared at myself. "What the heck, brain? We love tacos."

My reflection told me nothing, so I exited the bathroom and Shea immediately set his hands on my arms.

"Are you okay?"

"Sorry," I said with a nod. "The smell made me sick."

"We'll get something else delivered to the room. Come on, I'm taking you back to your room."

"But our date," I said with a pout.

"We can continue our date with me doting on you in your room," he said with a soft smile and kissed the top of my head. "Let me know immediately if you start to feel sick again."

As we gathered our things, I saw the rude woman had left already and her bracelet was still beneath the table. I grabbed it, hid it in my towel, and smirked. "We are on the high seas, so any booty lost belongs to the pirate who finds it."

"What?" Shea asked as he walked to me.

"Nothing," I said with a sweet smile. I glanced at our abandoned tacos and scowled. "Sorry, babies, but you're not good for me today."

Shea hovered at my side as we headed back to the room, ordered me into bed, and then went to talk to Stephan who'd looked on with a worried scowl.

"I'm really okay," I told Stephan as he watched me eat some spaghetti.

"Have that food tested," Stephan ordered Shea.

"Already in progress," Shea said.

My brows furrowed and I set my fork down. "Tested for what?"

"Poison," they said simultaneously.

"Would...would someone do that?" I asked, but I already knew the answer to that. Of course they would. If someone hated Stephan, they would definitely poison me to get at him.

"I've already been searching for a guard for her," Stephan said to Shea. "Come look at my suggestions."

Shea kissed the top of my head and left me to go with Stephan.

Well, poison wasn't something I'd thought of needing to deal with before, but now it was.

Yay for new problems.

CHAPTER TWELVE

"The doctor said he can't find anything wrong and it could just be a stomach bug," Shea said.

Dane sat at the end of the couch with my head on his lap and stroked my hair. "It could be," he agreed.

"I don't want to throw up anymore," I whined and rubbed my face on Dane's knee.

Shea sat at the opposite end of the couch, my feet in his lap while he rubbed them. "They're bringing anti-nausea medicine soon."

"This sucks. I'm sorry that I'm ruining your trip," I whined to the men who were all staring at me from around the room.

"You're not ruining our trip. We took this trip for you. We're just sad that you don't feel well," Arcadio said and squatted in front of me to pet my shoulder.

It was nighttime now and most of the other patrons were attending another ball event. I'd brought a dress to wear tonight, but that was clearly going to stay packed.

The lights flickered, which made all of the guys look up at the lights and then at each other.

"Feel anything?" Stephan asked softly. Everyone shook their heads.

Forrest walked over to flick the lock on the door, locking us inside.

"What's going on?" I asked.

"We aren't sure," Stephan answered and squinted as he tried to look out the window from the living room without getting closer.

"You think it's an attack," I realized.

"Incapacitate you, make us focus on your weakened form, and then attack to discombobulate us," Dane said. "Seems like a decent plan."

I reached over his knee, my hand going beneath the couch, and drew the gun I'd hidden there. "Stupid plan."

"What—" Stephan said.

"The—" Shea said.

"Shit—" Forrest said.

"Amelia!" Arcadio snapped.

After ensuring the safety was still on, I slid it back under the couch. "You guys act like I'm naïve, but I know that we need to be careful and there are a lot of people who would benefit from killing us, especially Stephan. When you told me I was rooming with him, I made sure to bring enough weapons to keep him safe."

Stephan rubbed his temples. "Keep me safe. This beautiful pain in my ass brought weapons to keep me safe."

The lights flickered again and then shut off. Immediately, the backup lights came on, their red hue eerie in the late night.

"Shea with Amelia," Stephan ordered.

Immediately, everyone went into action and I was too shocked at their coordinated movements to question it as they dispersed. Shea took me into his room and locked the door behind him.

After several long, silent moments, I looked at Shea who had his gun drawn and in his hand. "What's going on?"

"Attack of some sort," he answered. "You and I will stay here, only moving if the others tell us to."

"What if they go after Stephan?" I asked nervously.

"The others are staying with him," Shea answered.

"Why did we separate?"

"To ensure they can't catch us all at once. If Stephan and the others get captured, we'll go in after them," he explained.

"And if we get captured, they'll send one or two after us," I guessed with a nod. "Smart."

A woman screamed in the hallway and I stood, but Shea shook his head at me.

"I'm not going to just sit here while some poor woman is killed," I hissed at him.

He crowded into me, his shadow blocking out all of the light in the room. "My job is to keep you safe. No one else matters. In this moment, there is only you and me in this world. I don't care if some random person dies so long as you live."

"Shea," I whispered, "we can't let them get murdered. We have to help if we can." I put my hands on his chest and said, "We aren't the evil mafia crew people think we are. I understand keeping that persona for the other mafias, but we don't have to do that for the regular people we can keep from dying."

"Amelia," he grumbled.

"Either you're going to help me or I'm going to knock your ass out and leave you in here," I threatened him. With all of the adrenaline pumping through my veins, my nausea and other symptoms were gone.

He groaned. "You're going to be the death of me, Kitten."

I scoffed. "No, I won't. I'll disembowel anyone who tries to hurt you."

He moaned. "Don't say such sexy things when we've got no time for me to pleasure you."

I sucked in a breath. "Tease."

"Pretty sure that's what I just said," he muttered. "Stay behind me, finger in my belt loop, and give two tugs if you see something. Silence is key in these situations."

I nodded. "Understood."

"Stephan's going to kill me," he whispered, opened the door, and peeked his head out. "Clear," he whispered.

Following his orders, I walked behind him down the hallway and towards the sounds of frightened people.

We got to a corner and he stopped, holding a hand up behind him to let me know we needed to wait.

"You will put all of your jewelry, wallets, and other precious items into the bags. Failure to comply will mean immediate death," a man with a thick accent I couldn't place said.

"Then, you will put the wrist restraints on each other and a bag on the other's head," another man explained.

Shea pushed me back until we got to a side hallway, turned the knob on a room, and shoved me inside, clicking the lock into place. "Shit, they're kidnapping them." He started typing on his phone and I could see the deep scowl on his face as he typed.

"We need to stop them," I whispered. "If they get on that other ship, it's going to be over."

"They just want to use them for ransom," Shea muttered.

"Yes, but they'll kill several to ensure they get that ransom," I reminded him. It had happened several times over the last decade and had been all over the news channels every time.

He sighed and looked up at the ceiling for a long time, his mouth a thin line.

"Shea," I whispered when it didn't seem like he was going to speak.

"Yeah. I know, I know." He dropped his head to stare into my eyes. "You're my top priority. If some old man gets shot because I'm protecting you, I don't care."

"You're so sweet," I murmured and kissed his cheek. "Let's go."

His phone beeped, he scowled at it, opened his mouth, but I raised my hand.

"We didn't see the message so we're going into this on our own with no orders."

"He's going to punish you," he sang as he opened the door, gun ready.

I took my dagger out and smirked. "Promises. Promises."

He grunted before shaking his head and walking out of the room. We made our way down the hallway, back towards the room where the pirates had been gathering everyone, but it was now empty.

"Shit, they must have already gotten them. We'll need to head over and try to get them back on the cruise ship," Shea whispered.

Already ahead of him, I moved across the open room and towards the door on the far side that led out to the walkway. They'd likely set a temporary bridge across the two ships to get everyone across and that was where I was going.

"Amelia!" Shea hissed, but I was a woman on a mission and didn't stop.

"Hands up!" someone shouted behind me, but I had made it to the door and stepped out before they had time to shoot me.

The door clanged closed behind me, no one followed, and I realized that Shea had likely just been captured. No, not captured. My giant man would destroy anyone between me and him.

With that knowledge, I hurried across the unmanned bridge. The waves made the bridge move up and down and my throat constricted as fear gripped me. Squatting down to lower my center of mass, I edged across the bridge until I made it to the other ship.

Squatted by the back entrance beside the bridge, I took deep breaths to calm my racing heart and rising bile.

"Get the pictures!" a man yelled from within the door I stood beside. "We need to get it posted as soon as possible."

Shit. I needed to get those people out of there as soon as possible, but I wasn't certain how many enemies there were.

Staying squatted, I crept beneath the windows, around the back door, and to the other side where they'd be less likely to look for a woman snooping inside over the window edge.

Nose pressed to the glass, I watched the three men moving about the cabin inside as they kept the prisoners huddled together.

The old, rich people just sat together silently, no energy to try to riot.

This was going to be completely up to me and I was ridiculously excited about that.

With only three men to target, I went over the various possibilities and outcomes, preparing myself mentally for anything.

That was all interrupted when Shea, Forrest, and Dane burst inside, guns blasting, and killed the three men.

With them taken care of, my men on the job, I turned and ran up the stairs towards the bridge.

Two more men stood with guns aimed at two elderly men who were bound in metal handcuffs. They were likely the richest men on the ship and that's why they were being given extra special care.

Hip thrusting the door open, I shot the two kidnappers in their shocked faces and immediately ran over to take control of the ship.

"Who are you?" one of the elderly men asked, his voice raspy and weak.

"Stephan Moriarty's fiancée," I answered. "Keep quiet and let me handle this."

Keeping the boat steady, I listened to the radio communications coming in to determine the severity of the situation and see if there was anything we weren't aware of that we needed to be.

"Alright, let's get you back to the cruise ship," I said and turned to the elderly men who, surprisingly, had stayed kneeling on the ground behind me.

"You're not going to kill us?" one asked, his grey hair falling into his eyes.

Scowling I said, "Sir, Stephan Moriarty is a technology guru, not a thug. We don't kill people. Come on, I'm going to walk in front and shoot anyone who threatens us. You two stay behind me and get across the bridge as soon as you can. Understand?"

They both nodded and waited while I removed their cuffs before following me on silent feet.

How the two hobbling men were so stealthy was a mystery, but I accepted it and was glad for the break.

I got them onto the other ship and made it up to the bridge of our cruise ship with no problems.

As soon as I stepped into the cruise ship's bridge, three men pointed their guns at me.

I raised my hands up and smiled. "So sorry. I didn't realize this stall was taken."

"Who are you?" one of the men asked, his eyes narrowing as he took in my sweatpants and t-shirt. On the left side of his arm, I noticed a tattoo, one of two pigeons facing each other.

It was the symbol of a notorious pirate group with an incredibly stupid name: The Pigeonas.

"You give organized groups a terrible name," I told them as I lowered my arms. "Pigeons, really? Yuck."

They had all lowered their guns, surprised by my femininity and pathetic appearance.

With three quick pulls of the trigger, all three fell to the ground, dead before they could raise their guns back up.

Silence greeted me and I smiled. "Ah, silence is my favorite noise."

Humming to myself, I skipped to the controls to take over. Once our course was properly reset, I locked the doors to the bridge so no one could sneak in.

"How new are you that you don't even lock the door behind you?" I asked the three dead men on the floor. It really said something about how much had happened to me since joining the mafia that things like this no longer phased me. This was just another day in the life of a mobsterina.

A moment later, someone pounded on it.

I drew my gun, ready to shoot.

"Open up!" Shea ordered.

With a smirk, I opened the door. "Hey, handsome. Welcome to the party."

Shea, Dane, and Forrest gaped at me.

"Wait, you stole the ship?" Dane asked

"I don't know!" I shouted.

"How do you steal a ship and not know!" Forrest yelled.

"I don't know! It just happened, okay? I rescued a couple old men from the other boat and Shea was there so I figured he rescued the rest and came up here."

"So, you stole *two* ships?" Dane gaped. "Just when I thought you couldn't surprise me anymore, you become a pirate."

"Unintentionally!" I muttered.

"I swear I will tie you to my hip," Stephan hissed as he and Arcadio entered.

"Lock the door!" I ordered Arcadio.

He obeyed and then scowled at me. "Um, what?"

"The first thing you always do is secure all exits and entrances," I said and rolled my eyes. "You sure you're an assassin?"

He glared at me. "I know to keep my exits open to flee when needed."

"Status report," Stephan ordered and stepped up to my side, his eyes focused on the horizon.

"All the hostages have been recovered. I'm pretty certain we can just knock their makeshift bridge away and sail on," Forrest said.

"They're part of the Pigeonas," I explained. "They've got the tattoos."

Stephan rubbed his temples and sighed. "Those bastards have been a thorn in my side for years."

"Maybe it's time we eradicated them," Shea said.

"They did point their guns at me," I said. "I think that's a perfectly reasonable reason to destroy them."

"I want that ship destroyed," Stephan ordered. "Get their bodies on it before it explodes. The authorities will report it as a malfunction and our cruise will continue undeterred."

"You're pretty sexy when you take charge," I said and smiled up at him.

He slid his arm around my waist and pulled me against his chest. "Wait until someone threatens you in my territory."

I clenched my legs together and whimpered. "Tease."

"Radio it in. I want to resume our course and put this into our past as barely a memory," Stephan ordered them.

"Then we're going to eat ice cream!" I cheered.

They all looked at me curiously.

I shrugged one shoulder. "Every victory needs ice cream."

Stephan smiled. "I don't think anyone will complain about eating ice cream after being rescued."

"Oh snap!" I gasped.

They continued to stare at me.

"The enemy screamed for my ice cream!" I yelled.

Five groans sounded around me, but I couldn't stop smiling.

CHAPTER THIRTEEN

The cruise continued without any other issues, much to my disappointment.

When I returned to our house, Erina and Marlee both waited on the porch for me, one guard each next to them.

Hugs, squealing and gawking over my ring ensued before we hurried outside to the backyard to escape the guys.

"How did it happen? Tell us everything!" Erina ordered me.

After a recap of the proposal, I also gave them a recap of other events.

Immediately, they put their phones to their ears when they heard about the Pigeonas.

"What are you doing?" I hissed at them.

"Death list addition," Erina said when one of her men finally answered. "Pigeonas. Yes, the entire group."

"Baby, I need you to work with Connor to destroy the Pigeonas. Yes, that's what I said. Thank you. Bye."

My mouth stayed open as I stared at them.

"You didn't think we'd let that slide, did you?" Erina

scoffed. "Those assholes will be obliterated from this earth by tomorrow morning for threatening you and yours."

"Friends don't let friends have enemies," Marlee said with a serious nod.

"You two are the best bitches a girl like me could find," I said. Tears filled my eyes, and I sniffled.

Their arms wrapped around me as they squished me between them.

Erina pulled back, her mouth open. "Amelia!"

"What?" I asked.

She continued to stare at me.

"No!" Marlee screeched and took one of my hands in hers.

Used to their antics, I sighed and waited.

"Love, when was your last period?" Erina asked.

My brows furrowed. "Um, what?"

"I've got a test!" Marlee said and ran inside.

Erina pulled me into the house, grabbed Marlee's arm as she dug inside her purse, and we all went into the front bathroom.

Marlee finally found the plastic-wrapped item she was looking for. "Ah-ha!" She held out the pregnancy test. "We've been trying for a bit, so I've got a few I carry everywhere with me."

"Wait," I gasped and put my hands up. "No. No way!"

"Take it!" Marlee ordered me.

In a whispered hiss, Erina said, "Piss on that stick right now, Amelia. I thought you looked a bit different when you arrived, but put that on the engagement glow, but now I'm pretty sure that's not it."

"Oh boy. Whoa," I whispered as I walked to the toilet.

"Want us to leave?" Marlee asked.

I shook my head, not wanting to be alone. They turned their backs to give me some privacy.

After the most awkward pee session I'd ever had, I set the test on the sink, and the three of us stared.

"How long does it take?" I asked out the side of my mouth in a whisper. I wasn't sure why I whispered, but the moment seemed to need quiet.

"Two minutes," Marlee answered, turned away from the test, and then made me turn, too. "It's best not to look until the timer goes off."

"What are you three doing in the bathroom together?" Dane asked from outside.

I squeaked, feeling like a teenager caught smoking in the bathroom.

"I'm showing them my new butt tattoo," Erina lied smoothly.

There wasn't sound for a moment, so I thought he had walked away, but eventually, he whispered, "Okay," drawing the word out before his footsteps receded.

"Why do I feel like I'm doing something wrong?" I whisper-hissed.

"Because you are a good girl who doesn't like keeping secrets from her lovers. It's a great trait, but don't worry, we won't keep the news from them forever," Marlee said and patted my head.

"I want a tattoo," I whispered. "A peacock with bright colors and a glowing heart."

"Where would you get it?" Erina asked.

"My outer thigh, I think," I answered with a nod.

"That would be hot!" Marlee shouted. "I've got the perfect artist for it, too."

Erina's phone chimed, letting us know the timer was finished.

Swallowing hard, I turned but clenched my eyes closed at the last second. "I can't look! One of you tell me."

Erina took my left hand while Marlee took my right.

"Is there an answer you are hoping for?" Erina asked softly.

I shook my head. "We weren't trying, but I won't be sad if I am."

"Well, guess our celebration today has to be changed to cider because you've got a bun in your oven, baby," Erina whispered excitedly.

Marlee and Erina wrapped me up in hugs and we all jumped and squealed.

"Do you want us to leave?" Erina asked. "So you can tell them?"

"I'll tell them later," I said. "I want to get the wedding planning underway. Now that I know I'm expecting, I want to have this wedding in the next three months, before I get too noticeable."

Marlee's mouth dropped. "You want a wedding in three months?"

"We can have the private one at our new place and the public one at the hotel the guys own," I answered. "So, that helps with those major pieces."

"Let's go and start writing notes!" Erina said, a huge smile on her face. "I love planning weddings."

Marlee handed me the wrapper for the pregnancy test. "You should put that in here and hide it so the guys don't stumble upon it and freak out."

"Let's throw it away," I said. "I'm going to have our doctor come and give me another test just to be sure tonight. I'll message him while we start our wedding discussions."

Test properly thrown away, hands double-washed, we returned to the poolside and started making the decisions necessary.

Stephan and the others had vetoed neon colors but told me I could decide on everything else so long as they were allowed to choose which guests were invited.

I found it rude they vetoed *all* neon colors, but I could work around that.

"I would keep the colors the same for both weddings so you don't have to buy new stuff," Erina said as she pulled out the binder she'd brought over.

They'd purchased a planner, but had quickly decided it wasn't good enough, ripped out pages they liked, created new ones, and made a frankenplanner.

"Budget?" Marlee asked.

She looked at me and simultaneously, Erina, Marlee and I burst into laughter.

"Let's keep it under a billion total for both," Stephan said as he walked out of the sliding glass door.

"Hey, Stephan," Erina and Marlee greeted with smirks.

He dipped his head and kissed my cheek. "You feeling better today?"

"Actually, I was about to message the doctor to ask him to stop by," I admitted and bit my lip.

His eyes widened. "Do we need to go to the hospital? I'll call a chopper."

He had his phone up to his ear in an instant, so I quickly grabbed his arm and pulled it down. "No! Stephan, it's okay. I just wanted the doctor to come by and run a couple tests. Is that okay? I didn't think you would mind me being extra cautious."

He rested his hand on my cheek and said, "You can run whatever test you want if it will put your mind at ease. Do you want me to call him?"

I shook my head with a smile. "It's okay. I can handle it. Erina and Marlee are doing all the note writing for the wedding. I'm just providing answers. So, I can message the doctor and answer their questions at the same time."

"If you need *anything*, let me know," he said. "I'll hire a live-in nurse if you need one."

My cheeks flushed and I didn't miss Erina and Marlee staring like lovesick puppies at us. "I'm okay. I'll just message the doc and get him to come over tonight. Okay?"

He nodded to me, nodded to the girls, and went back into the house.

"Oh. My. God," Marlee exclaimed.

Erina fanned herself. "My boys better step up their games or I might try and steal that man."

Narrowing my eyes, I said, "Mine. You can't have him."

She laughed. "Fine. Let's get back to your wedding. So, what color are we going with?"

"No neon colors," I grumbled and folded my arms across my chest.

"Any flower preference?" Marlee asked.

"I like star-shaped flowers mainly," I admitted. "And lilies."

"Purple!" Marlee shouted.

Erina and I looked at her with wide eyes.

Marlee blushed a bit. "Purple would be the perfect color for her wedding."

"Bright purple, *almost* neon," I said with a wicked smile.

"Magenta!" Marlee and Erina said at the same time and then burst into laughter.

"Perfect!" I agreed.

"Do you have any wedding dress ideas?" Erina asked as she made some notes.

I nodded and opened my cell phone to the Bravard's Bridal site where I had favorited a bunch of styles. "Here."

Erina and Marlee huddled together as they swiped through my favorites.

"We'll schedule an appointment for next weekend," Erina said and pulled out her own phone.

"You're making me get a designer dress from your designer, aren't you?" I asked, not sure if I should pout or kiss her feet.

She smirked. "You learn fast. Faster than my boys." The second sentence was mumbled and made me laugh.

"Okay, take this paper and write down your family members' names, emails, phone numbers, and addresses if you know them," Marlee ordered me.

I took my phone back, remembered to message the doctor who immediately replied he would be over in two hours, and then did as she asked. It was a short list anyway.

"That's it?" she asked and Erina's eyebrows rose when she looked over Marlee's shoulder.

I shrugged. "I don't have much family."

"Okay, well that makes it easier," Marlee said.

"What about the guys?" Erina asked.

I tensed and gnawed on my lower lip. We hadn't really talked about their families much since they never visited them. I did know that some of their families were mostly dead, but I wasn't one hundred percent certain. "I'm...not sure," I admitted.

"We'll have them fill out the list, don't worry," Erina said with a soft smile.

After another hour of wedding planning, we wrapped things up with to-do's for each of us to meet up in three days to do more work.

"Text us immediately!" Erina ordered me.

I nodded and smiled softly. "You got it."

As soon as I shut the door, Shea's deep male voice asked, "Text them about what?"

Not screaming was the greatest feat I'd pulled off in a year. Hand to my chest, I turned around to glare at him but found all five men standing in the living room behind me. "Uh…"

"Want to explain why the doctor is at the gate?" Forrest asked.

I looked at Stephan. "Didn't you tell them?"

"I told them, but they seem to think you're withholding something," he said and shrugged. "Something about the way your upper lip moves when you speak."

Arcadio smirked at me. "It's a tell, Sweets."

I'd show him sweet. "You guys are so paranoid."

The doorbell rang and even though I was the closest, Arcadio beat me to the door to let the doctor in.

Dr. Augustus Tavian dipped his head to Arcadio before smiling at me. "Amelia, dear, let's go to your room."

"Okay," I agreed with a smile and a nod.

He put a hand on my lower back and steered me down the hallway, but paused halfway down, turning around to glare. "No! You all go out to the pool area or I'll take her to the office. I'm not going to have you breathing down our necks or making her uncomfortable."

Dane opened his mouth, but Stephan interrupted.

"He's right. Let's go outside and talk, boys," Stephan ordered, his tone brokering no room for argument.

Once in my room with the door closed, I exhaled harshly and smiled at Dr. Tavian. "Thank you."

He patted my shoulder and sat in the office chair. "So, tell me what's got you asking me here? Stephan said you were sick on the ship and that you might have caught a stomach bug."

"A stomach bug, all right," I muttered, which had the doc cocking a brow. With a deep breath, I said, "I need you to give me a pregnancy test."

To his credit, he didn't widen his eyes or act surprised. He nodded, opened his bag, and pulled out a few items, one being an empty plastic cup with a lid. "Pee in this, please, and then leave it in the bathroom."

I did as he said and returned to my room.

He went into the bathroom and I tried hard to calm my racing heart, but it would not stop.

"The results are positive," he said as he returned. "If you are planning on keeping it, we'll need to schedule an ultrasound for ultimate confirmation and to determine how far along you are. If you want other options—"

"I'm keeping it," I blurted.

He smiled. "Wonderful. Then we'll need to schedule your appointments; in the next few days I would like you to come to my office to have the ultrasound and have some blood tests done to ensure you're healthy and there are no abnormalities. I assume you plan to inform the gentlemen as they're going to hound me relentlessly until you explain your call tonight. I will not disclose your health to them as that would be a breach of confidentiality, so if you do not want to tell them, then I'd like us to agree on a diagnosis I can tell them."

"You really are the best doctor," I praised. "It's okay. I plan to tell them as soon as you leave."

He nodded. "Great. Are you available tomorrow afternoon for the ultrasound?"

"Yes, I could get to your office by four o'clock," I said as I thought about work and traffic.

"Perfect. I'll have everything ready when you arrive," he said and pulled out a small bottle. "I brought you some anti-nausea pills, too. Oh, and you'll want to buy some prenatal vitamins. You can get them at the grocery store."

I walked him out and then walked out to the backyard where the guys sat around on the patio furniture, each with a drink in hand.

I took a moment to enjoy seeing them sitting together in the moonlight. These men were my everything. Getting married wasn't something I'd expected when we had started dating, but it was something I had admittedly craved. Now, knowing we were going to bring another being into the world together, almost had me tearing up.

Dane stood and asked, "Do you want me to get you a drink or something to eat?"

I shook my head, smiled, and said, "Sit, please."

Dane sat, scowling, and all of them stared at me.

With a huge smile I broke it to them as quickly as I could. "I'm pregnant."

CHAPTER FOURTEEN

"I'm sorry…can you repeat that?" Dane asked.

"We're doing an ultrasound tomorrow for final confirmation, but I took an at-home test that Marlee had and then the doc gave me one when he came, too. I am pregnant."

"And…you want to keep it, right? That's why you're doing the ultrasound tomorrow?" Forrest asked, up on his feet and moving closer to me.

I nodded. "Yes, I am keeping it."

Forrest wrapped his arms around me and squeezed gently, his nose nuzzling into my hair. "I'm so happy."

Shea dropped to his knees and pressed his hands to my stomach. "A baby? We're having a baby?"

Dane set his hand on my cheek, smiled, and kissed me. "That's great, Babe."

"This calls for a sugary sweet celebration!" Stephan said with a wide smile. He walked over and kissed my cheek. "Is that why you worked so hard on the wedding today? To hold it before you have the baby?"

I nodded. "Yeah, I want to have it within the next three months so I won't be showing yet. Is that okay?"

"We'll do whatever you want," he said. "What do you want to eat?"

"Ice cream sundaes!" I shouted, which made Dane chuckle.

As they began ordering their sundaes, I realized Arcadio had disappeared.

Instead of assuming the worst, I headed into the house and to the kitchen where I could hear glass clinking. He stood at the counter downing a shot of whiskey and immediately refilled the glass.

"I left so I wouldn't spoil everyone's happy mood," he said without turning around.

"You don't want kids?" I asked, no judgment in my tone.

"I love kids and have always wanted kids," he said. "I...I can't have kids, though." The words were almost a broken whisper and it tore my heart apart.

I wrapped my arms around his waist and rested my head between his shoulder blades. "I'm sorry."

"I'm happy for you and I'll spoil the shit out of this kid, but it just hurts knowing there is absolutely no possible way it is mine genetically." He sighed, spun around, and hugged me tight. "I sound like an asshole; I don't care whose kid it is, because it will be yours, but it's different knowing it could be mine and knowing with one hundred percent certainty that it isn't."

"I get it," I whispered. "I'm sorry, Arcadio."

"Go on. Go back out there and celebrate," he said with a sniffle.

I shook my head against his chest. "I don't want to leave you alone."

"What kind of ice cream you want for your sundae?" Dane asked from the doorway.

"I'm good," Arcadio said.

"Amelia!" Stephan called.

I looked up at Arcadio and he smiled down at me, rested his hand on my cheek, and said, "Go. You can't ignore a direct order from the boss. Not without punishment."

"Go on," Dane ordered. "Don't make him call you again."

I sighed, grabbed Arcadio's face, pulled him down, and kissed him like it was the first time. He pressed against me, falling into the kiss. I pulled back with a gasp and panted a bit before turning and walking out of the kitchen.

Stephan scowled at me. "You okay?"

I nodded. "Yeah."

"We were talking about the new place," he commented. "We think we need to make some adjustments to the room situation now that we know we are expecting another permanent member."

That hadn't even occurred to me yet.

"Uh, right. We'll need a room to use as a nursery and then as their room. Unless we want one that's the nursery and then move them when they get older?" Raising kids was so not something I had thought about yet.

"Let's just assign them a nursery for now and maybe when they get older, they can request a room change then," Stephan said with a slight smile.

I nodded. "Okay, let me go grab my tablet so we can review the floor plans."

"You just stay here and I'll get your tablet," Shea ordered me.

With hands on my hips, I glared up at the giant. "I am not

an invalid just because I'm pregnant, sir. I can still walk to my damn room and back."

"Don't test me, Amelia, or I'll carry you everywhere," he grumbled and stomped away.

My mouth dropped as I watched him walk away.

Stephan chuckled. "Don't worry, I'll talk with them. Deep breath, Darling."

"I need to schedule a cake taste-test as soon as possible," I informed Stephan and pulled out my cell phone. As soon as I pulled it out, I remembered I needed to text Erina and Marlee. I remembered because there were a dozen messages in our shared chat.

"What are you smirking about?" Forrest asked.

"Erina and Marlee are worried about how you'll respond to my news," I said.

The tension in the room quadrupled as Dane, Arcadio, and Shea returned at the moment I said that.

"Wait…" Dane whispered.

"They knew…" Arcadio added.

"Before us!" Shea snapped.

"They're the ones who suspected and Marlee had a test," I explained. "I didn't even think about it being a possibility."

"You really find it surprising that her girlfriends would be the first she would discuss a womanly problem with?" Stephan asked with folded arms. "You boys are out of the know."

"So, anyway, um, how long until sundaes are here?" I asked with a wide smile.

Shea held out my tablet. "Can you sit on the couch?"

I narrowed my eyes up at him.

He sighed. "Please?"

With a wide smile, I sat next to Forrest and said, "Certainly!"

As we looked through the floor plans, I started to gnaw on my lower lip. It was hard to decide where I wanted my room in conjunction to the guys'.

"Hand it over," Stephan ordered.

I obeyed, reluctantly.

He crossed one ankle over the other knee, rested the tablet on his bent knee, and tapped his chin while he looked at the rooms.

He had said he wanted us to move forward in our relationship and that included being able to cuddle and hold hands. Would he mind if I scooted closer and leaned against him?

Deciding to test that out, I scooted over until our hips were just an inch apart, but then froze, suddenly too nervous about leaning over.

He lifted the arm that was between us, draped it around my shoulders, and tugged me closer. "No need to get stage fright, Darling."

With a sigh, I rested my head against his arm, looked down at my gorgeous ring, and said, "Everything's just happening so fast."

Stephan patted my arm. "Although it isn't completely ideal, it'll be okay."

My phone rang and I cringed when I saw my mom's name on the caller ID. "Well, I guess it's time I took care of this," I whispered. With a deep breath, I answered and immediately put the phone on speaker. "Hi, Mom!"

"Don't you start with me, Amelia! I should kick your ass nine days to Wednesday for this new stunt. What in Saint Jimmy's Christmas is wrong with you?" My mom's voice had a slight accent to it, which meant she'd been spending a lot of time in the South with her family. "You know how I found out? I found out at church with your nana sitting beside me, from that tart, Anna Beth! You know I can't stand that woman. She uses canned cranberries for crying cicadas. Bless her heart."

"Mom, I have something to tell you," I said.

"I should say so! Getting engaged to some rich, hoity-toity, egotistical, self-important, scumbag who likely has a judge or two in his pocket," she huffed.

Stephan's brows rose as he stared at the phone.

"Elizabeth Sarah!" I snapped. "You be nice."

She sighed. "Fine, tell me your news and then I'll actually speak my mind."

"Actually?" Dane asked softly behind me.

"No, you know what, Mom? This requires an in-person visit. Where are you at?" I asked. "I'll fly out tomorrow evening."

"You can't fly," Shea whispered-hissed in my ear.

I turned a glare on him that had his hands immediately up in the air and him backing away.

"I'm at Aunt Judith's," Mom answered.

Aunt Judith lived in one of the smallest cities in the country. It would require a two-hour flight, a twenty-minute bus to the car rental place, and another three-hour drive just to get there.

"The Blain B&B still open?" I asked.

She snorted. "Duh."

"Anyone in it this week?" I asked.

"Just me and the boys," she answered.

That meant there were three rooms taken, which left four more available.

"Mom, I'm going to mute you real quick so give me a second," I ordered her.

"A year with some rich man and she's suddenly more important than me," Mom huffed, but went quiet.

Rolling my eyes, I muted her, exhaled harshly, and said, "I have a favor to ask."

"Arcadio and I will stay here to take care of the business while you and the others go," Stephan said.

I shook my head. "I really need you to come. Please. I know this is a lot to ask after I just took you away on this cruise."

"Need or want?" he asked.

His tone had changed when he asked that so I took a moment to consider. "Both, actually."

He nodded. "Shea and Arcadio will stay and tend to the business while the rest of us go to meet your mother."

"Why us?" Shea asked.

"I'm confident you two can handle any issues that have arisen or that will arise in our continued absence," Stephan said. "Especially any that pertain to the mafia side."

Arcadio smiled. "That means I get to have some fun."

Stephan narrowed his eyes. "Jackal…"

Arcadio raised his hands and laughed. "I was teasing."

"We can leave after my appointment tomorrow with the doctor?" I asked.

Stephan nodded. "Yes."

Unmuting my mother again, I said, "Alright, Mom, I need the rest of the Blain B&B's rooms. We will arrive tomorrow night, okay?"

"Really? You're coming to see me?" she asked and screamed loudly.

"What is it?" Randolph, one of my mom's boyfriends, asked.

"My baby is coming to see me!" Mom screamed.

"I'm still here," I said and shook my head with a wide smile. "I love you, Mom. I'll see you tomorrow."

"Love you, too. We'll keep the light on."

She hung up and I dropped back against Stephan, covering my face with my hands. "What did I just agree to? Now you'll meet my family and call off the wedding."

He kissed the top of my head and said, "Your mom sounds fun, just like you are. I'm sure we're going to have a lot of fun. Here, look at the room arrangements I made and let me know your thoughts."

"Sundaes are here," Dane said and walked towards the door.

"I need a drink," I muttered, then remembered I couldn't drink anymore and fake cried.

"She just remembered she has to drink virgin drinks for the next year," Arcadio said with a chuckle.

I groaned as the length of time was said and Stephan patted my back. "Let's go and enjoy our ice cream. Ice cream makes everything better."

"I need extra whipped cream," I ordered Forrest.

He smiled wide and said, "I'm pretty sure that's what got you into this situation in the first place."

A bark of laughter escaped me at his joke and then I doubled over in laughter, arms wrapped around my stomach as I laughed until I cried.

"I love you all."

My leg bouncing had quadrupled from the flight to the car ride and I definitely shook the entire SUV as we drove closer to my mom.

"You sure we're going the right way?" Dane asked as he watched the empty fields out the window. It was starting to get dark, which made it harder to see how far the fields spanned.

"Yep. The farther we get from the city, the closer we get to their small town."

"Why are you so nervous?" Forrest asked. "Your mom is poly, so it's not like she won't understand you becoming poly, right?"

I wasn't certain. Mom had a track record of doing one thing herself, but judging others for doing it.

"I'm not here for her approval," I explained. "I'm here to tell her in person that she's going to be a grandmother. That's all."

"Everything will be okay," Stephan assured me from the front passenger seat. "This will be the perfect opportunity to personally invite her to our wedding, too."

"Speaking of weddings and families, did you guys send your lists to Erina yet?" I asked to change the subject a little and distract myself.

"Yes," Stephan answered. "We compiled it all into one list and sent it to her."

"Awesome," I replied with a smile.

"We also have a surprise for you tonight, once we all have some alone time," Dane said, smiling wide.

"I hate surprises and you know that. You're so cruel."

He chuckled. "Trust me, this will be worth the wait."

Things with them normally were.

An hour later, we finally saw the first building of the town.

"We're here," I breathed.

"This is straight out of a small-town romance movie," Forrest commented as we passed through the town square.

"They've filmed several of them here, actually," I said. The town used it to their advantage when putting up advertisements. People flocked here during the snowy season to take pictures from scenes in their favorite movies.

We drove past all the familiar places until we reached the most adorable bed-and-breakfast Victorian house with a long, curved driveway lined by weeping willows. The house was painted a nice shade of lavender and was extremely well taken care of. The electrical had been completely redone to match current codes, while keeping the same fixtures and ensuring minimal visibility to those who visited. When you entered the grounds, it was like you were transported back fifty years. They even offered tea throughout the day in centuries old teacups.

At the front porch stood my mother, her hair was braided tightly against her head, her summer dress had pretty flowers on it, and in her hands was a steel bat.

"What's the bat for?" Stephan asked.

I gulped. "When I get out, you all need to stay in the car until I say so, okay?"

"What?" they all asked.

The car stopped, I hopped out, and Mom swung the bat at my head.

I ducked the swing, slipped on the gravel, and landed on my butt.

She reversed her swing, but paused when she saw me on the ground. "Are you that out of practice?"

I huffed, stood, and dusted off my pants. "I haven't fought on gravel in a decade, Mom."

"You okay?" Dane asked, rushed to me, and ran his hands over me.

"I'm fine," I assured him, a little miffed he hadn't listened to me, but glad they hadn't immediately tackled my mom.

He looked down at my stomach with a scowl and I could tell he was worried about the baby.

"Dane, I just slipped and fell on my butt. I'm *fine. Everything* is fine."

He nodded and stepped back to let Stephan come to my side who frowned down at me, but said nothing.

"Mom, can we talk inside?" I asked.

Just out of the corner of my eye, I could see the town's most gossipy women sipping tea on the balcony and pretending they weren't watching us.

She nodded, turned, and led us into the bed-and-breakfast, up the stairs, and into her room where Randolph sat in a recliner reading a thick paperback book. He looked up when we entered, stood, and then glared at the men over my head. "What's all this?"

I hurried over, hugged him, and said, "I'll explain everything once we're all inside and the door and window are shut."

He immediately shut the window while Forrest shut the door behind everyone.

Mom set the bat on the end of the bed, put her hands on her hips, and said, "Spill it."

"First, Mom, I know you heard about my engagement to Stephan, but that's not the full story," I explained.

"Which one is Stephan?" she asked as she scanned the guys. "They all look a bit hoity-toity."

"Eli, be nice," Randolph warned her.

"Right, introductions first," I said.

Stephan stepped forward, held out his hand to my mom,

and said, "I'm Stephan Moriarty. It's a pleasure to meet my fiancée's mother finally."

Mom shook his hand and smiled wide. "It's nice to meet you, too. Such a gentleman. I can see why my daughter likes you."

"This is Dane and Forrest, they're Stephan's right-hand men," I explained.

She shook their hands and exchanged pleasantries with them, too.

"There's also Shea and Arcadio, but they're holding down the fort while we're here," I added. "And, that ends my introduction of the men in my harem." While I wasn't a fan of the term harem, it was one my mom loved to use to describe her version of polyamory. Most polyamorous relationships didn't limit either sex's ability to date others, but since she, and I, were jealous jerks we didn't want our men dating others. So, calling them a harem was more fitting.

Mom's brows shot up into her hairline. "You made your own harem? But you said you would never be able to do that."

I shrugged. "Guess the apple really doesn't fall far from the tree."

Her laughter as she tossed her head back, echoed around the small room. "I always knew one man wouldn't be enough to handle you," Mom said once she'd finished laughing.

"Our wedding will be in three months," I went on like she hadn't made that comment. "And of course, you are invited, as are all of your men."

"Like you could keep me away," she said with a wide smile.

"I don't have invitations printed yet, so I'll mail it to you," I added.

"Why are you doing it so soon?" Randolph asked, his eyes narrowed suspiciously.

"Can you sit a second?" I requested.

Randolph and Mom sat on the end of the bed.

"The main reason I came here wasn't to invite you to the wedding or even introduce you to the guys. It was to tell you that you're going to be a grandma." I blurted it so fast that I wasn't sure she even understood what I said.

Her blank stare made me open my mouth to repeat it, but then her eyes widened, she leaped up, threw her arms around me, and screamed joyfully.

When she released me, Dane held out the copy of the ultrasound we'd had printed for her.

She took it gingerly, like she was afraid she could break it. "My first grandbaby."

"I don't want to jinx it, but their current due date is your birthday," I whispered with a small smile.

She dropped to her knees and we all reached out towards her, but then she scooted closer to me, pressed the side of her face to my belly, and said, "I'm going to teach you all the things your momma sucks at."

Tears slipped down my cheeks as I sniffled. "You suck at more things than me. You can't even thread a needle."

"Just ignore her," Mom whispered. "We're going to be the best of friends and whenever you come over, I'm going to take you shooting and show you the proper way to bake chocolate chip cookies."

"I still make better cupcakes than you can," I grumbled. "My frosting is far superior to yours."

"Maybe you'll be able to use a crossbow. Your momma is pretty useless with one," Mom continued.

"I'm better now!" I protested and then stepped back. "Okay, enough buttering up the baby. It doesn't even have ears yet."

She returned to sitting on the bed beside Randolph and looked at the guys. "You know which one is the biological father?"

I shook my head. "No, and I don't intend to find out."

"Whose name will you put as the father?" she asked and tilted her head sideways.

"Mine," Stephan answered immediately. "I have the biggest fortune for the child to inherit and while I'm definitely not the biological father, I will be the one legally married to Amelia as well."

"You know for certain it isn't yours?" Mom asked, her brows furrowed.

"We haven't slept together," I answered before Stephan could say anything.

Mom smirked. "Ah, I see. Well, it sounds like you've got this all planned out. I'm glad she found partners who can help her sort her life out. There was a period of time I worried every time the phone rang that it would be the cops asking me to identify her corpse."

"Or bail me out," I added.

She chuckled. "Or that."

"We're glad we were able to find someone who fit our dynamic so well," Dane said, slipped his arm around my waist, and tugged me against his side with a smile. "She's perfect."

"Definitely not perfect, but pretty close," Forrest added as he came to stand on my other side and smiled down at me.

"They look like us twenty years ago," Randolph said, smiled wide, and bumped his shoulder into Mom's.

She chuckled. "Except none of my boys have those sexy dimples. I always tried to find one, but it seems my girl snagged two to make up for it."

I rolled my eyes. "Yes, that's why."

"Alright, let's get you situated in your rooms and then we can go eat dinner," Mom said and stood.

She showed us to the rooms, then stepped into Stephan's room and shut the door behind her.

"Uh oh," I whispered.

"Come on, gorgeous, you're bunking with me tonight," Forrest said. "We can change before we eat dinner and talk with your mom more."

I chewed on my lip nervously, wondering what my mother was talking to Stephan about, but obeyed Forrest. Once we changed into more comfortable clothing, we met the others back outside on the porch.

I was glad to see Anna Beth and her two cousins had vacated the premises so we had it to ourselves.

Forrest pulled out my chair for me and kissed my cheek before he sat. "You really look gorgeous lately. I guess there really is a pregnancy glow."

"Shush," I hushed him. "We can't discuss that publicly. There are always snoopy bitches sneaking around in this town."

"Not tonight," Dane said as he stepped out of the shadows to join us. "I did a full perimeter sweep."

"You know," I said with a smirk. "Since I'm already knocked up, we can do it as much as we want."

They looked at each other and then at me, a silent communication having passed between each other in that moment.

"Down girl!" Mom said as she joined us. "Though, to be honest, I was much hornier when I was pregnant, so I don't blame you."

I narrowed my eyes. "Please don't talk to me about your sex life, Mother."

She smirked. "Fine. Fine."

Stephan joined us a moment later with Randolph at his side, both whispering conspiratorially.

"That makes me nervous to see," I mumbled.

Mom just continued smirking.

"So, you're engaged, knocked up, and working for an IT company," Mom said. "What else is new?"

"Oh, I joined a mafia," I said with a nod.

Mom's eyes narrowed. "Again?"

"Would you believe this was by accident…again?"

She sighed, closed her eyes, and rubbed her temples. "She's going to be the death of me, Randolph."

"Technically, she lost a bet and that's how she joined," Forrest supplied.

Mom's head snapped up, her eyes wide. "Wait…you…"

I nodded. "It's hush-hush, but yes."

"Whatever happened with that loser? The one whose leg you broke?" Mom asked.

"I killed him," Stephan answered as he took a seat beside me, a shit-eating grin on his face.

"Good," Mom praised.

"I also made friends with two other mafia boss' wives. You'll love them, they're definitely your type," I said and smiled wide.

"How was your cruise?" she asked.

"Wait…" I narrowed my eyes. "How'd you know about my cruise?"

She smiled, picked up the teacup in front of her, and said, "You told me, silly."

I most certainly had not.

Turning my glare on Randolph, he shifted uncomfortably. "You're stalking me?"

He shifted from foot to foot and then sighed. "She made me!"

"Whoa, are you saying you were able to find out she was taking a cruise without her telling you?" Forrest asked. "How?"

Randolph shrugged. "I've got a lot of feelers out there for her name. I have to make sure a hit isn't put on the dark web again."

"Again?" Stephan and Dane shouted at the same time.

I waved my hand dismissively. "That was one time and that guy disappeared along with that hit request."

Stephan blinked at me, tilted his head sideways, and stared in silence.

"What the hell, Amelia?" Dane grunted and dropped his head until his forehead hit the top of the table. "I think I'm having a heart attack."

Mom patted his back. "That's just acid reflux. Keep some Tums on you, and you'll be fine. She has that effect on people."

"You look so innocent and then...I keep learning so much about you," Stephan said. "You are truly remarkable."

"Infuriating, Stephan. Not remarkable," Dane said, his head still on the table.

"Stop being dramatic," I said with a snort and rolled my eyes.

"Your snacks," RJ, the owner of Blain B&B said as she set a tray of cheeses, crackers, and meats on the table before us. She was short, had light-brown hair, and a face that didn't seem to age. She was well over thirty and yet constantly got carded for alcohol.

"Thanks, RJ," I said with a wide smile.

She winked. "Good to see you, girl." She looked at the guys next to me. "Come by whenever you want."

Mom snickered softly as she grabbed some cheeses.

"I'm impressed you've kept your mafia side and tech side separate," Randolph commented as he filled his plate, too.

"It hasn't been easy," Stephan admitted, chewing on a piece of cheese. "I've paid quite a few people off over the past decade."

"I bet," Randolph said with a nod.

"Where are the rest of your men?" I asked my mom.

She sighed. "Had a bit of a falling out with Dart and Lark."

"They'll be back," Randolph said confidently. "They just get scared when we start talking about doing illegal things."

I choked and both Stephan and Dane smacked my back. "What illegal things?" I rasped before chugging water.

"I was just checking up on you," she grumbled. "They didn't like that I'd hacked into Moriarty Tech files."

It was Stephan's turn to choke. "What?"

"Oh, right. Sorry," Mom said and shrugged a shoulder. "Your firewalls are pretty easy, by the way."

Stephan had his phone to his ear in an instant. "What the fuck, Ox?"

I couldn't hear Shea, but I could guess his confusion.

Stephan put him on speakerphone. "Elizabeth, would you be so kind as to explain why I've called my head of security?"

"I cracked your firewalls in three minutes," Mom said simply. "Beef them up, toots."

"Toots?" I asked and Mom shrugged.

"Why am I not surprised that Amelia's mother broke into our database?" Shea muttered.

"I heard that, Ox!" I snapped.

"Love you!" he called out and then hung up.

"Insufferable giant," I muttered and popped a cherry tomato into my mouth.

"Anything else we should know?" Stephan asked.

"Oh, I hacked your security footage," Randolph said. "Don't feel bad, though. I was trained by the Government to do it. Your security is pretty good, but I was able to do it."

Stephan groaned and dropped his head back to look up at the night sky. "Terrible. My security is terrible."

"Randolph provides consultant services," I supplied. "He could help you guys fix the holes."

Stephan turned to Randolph and the negotiations immediately started.

"Are you leaving tomorrow?" Mom asked.

I nodded. "We need to get back to work. We were off for the cruise and can't be gone much longer."

She smiled, softer than usual. "Thank you for coming to deliver this news in person. I appreciate it."

I winked. "You betcha."

"Now, who wants to play cards?" Mom asked and rubbed her hands together.

"Don't take all their money," I ordered her. "We need some for breakfast before we leave."

She smiled. "I'll buy breakfast."

"You think she's going to beat us?" Dane asked.

I shrugged. "It's your wallet. Have fun."

"Alright, what's your poison?" she asked as she pulled a deck out of her pants, shuffled, and bridged without even looking at the cards.

"Oh my," Stephan whispered.

I snickered. "This is going to get good."

"We could play strip poker?" Mom suggested and winked at me.

"You…you wrote your bucket lists?" I asked. We sat in Stephan's room in the bed-and-breakfast, huddled together on the floor. The guys had lost all of the cash they'd brought in their wallets to my mom and we'd retired to the room.

"Yes," Stephan answered. "We spent several hours on this topic to ensure we had realistic and good lists and not just ones we threw together for you."

Tears built in my eyes. "You guys…"

I couldn't even finish my sentence.

Dane kissed my cheek. "Don't cry. This is supposed to make you happy.

"It does make me happy," I said and sniffled. "So, let me hear 'em. Tell me your bucket lists."

"I'll go first," Stephan said. "I want to lay in a field of flowers on a warm, sunny day. I want to go camping, legitimate camping in a tent with no extra amenities. I want to go shopping at a regular grocery store." I opened my mouth to interrupt, but he glared at me, so I snapped my mouth closed. "I want to go to a normal, average nightclub. And, I want to see Amelia as an old lady with grey hair."

The last one had me choked up again.

"My turn," Dane said. "I want to visit Stonehenge. See the Aurora Borealis, and see the Golden Gate Bridge. Drive down Highway 1. And see our children as rebellious teenagers."

"Are you all trying to make me cry?" I whispered.

"Mine aren't as interesting," Shea said. "I want to buy you something that makes you cry as soon as you see it. I want to go to Tokyo, and I want to see you in a maid outfit."

"I have to admit," I whispered. "I'm honestly surprised by most of your items. You guys really did take your time to think about them. Thank you."

Shea knelt before me. "We'd do almost anything you asked us to, Kitten. Seriously, say the word and I'll do it."

"Stab Dane," I said.

Shea pulled a knife from his belt and I had to grab his arm, laughter making it hard to stop him. "I was joking," I gasped between laughs.

"Super rude," Dane grumbled and crossed his arms.

"He's right, though," Stephan said. "We love you, darling, and will do pretty much anything you want. Keep that in mind when you ask things of us in the future."

"Am I allowed to plan bucket-list trips?" I asked. "Like, the close ones we can mark off that don't require overnight stays and stuff?"

Stephan nodded. "Yes."

"Did the others make lists, too?" I asked. There were several trips we could take that would mark off multiple items from several lists at the same time.

"Within reason," Stephan said.

"This is seriously the best gift any of you could have given me. Thank you."

"So, when do we get to see your full list?" Shea asked.

I smiled wide. "When we get home. It's only two hundred and eighty items long."

Their shocked faces had me laughing all the way to the bathroom.

CHAPTER FIFTEEN

Saying goodbye to my mom was harder than I thought it would be. She clung to me and sniffled, but didn't cry.

"I'll be there two days before the wedding to help with final preparations," Mom said.

I nodded and smiled. "Great! See you then."

Most of the trip home was quiet, only interrupted when the guys would whisper to each other. Exhaustion hit me hard as we returned and I chalked it up to finally seeing my mom and telling her everything.

Stephan said it was common in the first trimester as well.

The next few months flew by; we all returned to work, but I'd had the added responsibilities of preparing for the wedding and planning out the enhancements to our new places.

As I stared at my reflection in the mirror while the designer made final tweaks to the dress, it felt like I was dreaming.

"Don't you dare try to run," Erina snarled at me from where she sat, the makeup artist doing her makeup.

"That's not at all what I was thinking," I said with a chuckle.

"Done!" the designer announced and smiled as she looked at me. "Perfection."

"Thank you for coming today," I said with a sincere smile. "You really didn't have to come."

She scoffed. "And miss the wedding of the decade? No, thank you for allowing me to attend the wedding of Stephan Moriarty. This is going to triple my orders."

"You'd better still make time for us," Erina said.

"You three are the top of my list," she promised, waved, and went to join the rest of the attendees.

"How are you feeling?" Marlee asked, the dress she'd ordered hugged her curves and showed just enough cleavage to be tasteful, but sexy.

"Good," I replied honestly. "Nervous because I don't want to trip or embarrass myself in front of so many people."

"That's why we got you flat shoes," Erina teased and stood, the makeup artist finally done.

"Can you take a picture of us?" I requested before the makeup artist could leave.

She smiled. "Of course!"

Erina handed her phone over and then came to stand at my side. Marlee stood on my other side and both slid their arms around my waist.

"Thank you both for being the best friends a girl could have. I won't say more because I don't want to ruin our wonderful artist's work, but thank you," I whispered.

"Love you," Erina said and squeezed my side.

"Ditto," Marlee said with a chuckle.

"Smile!"

We all smiled and posed.

"Ready?" Marlee asked as we all smoothed our dresses down.

I nodded, a huge smile on my face. "Yes. Yes, I am."

Erina opened the door and Mom's eyes immediately teared up.

"No!" I shouted. "Don't you dare cry!"

She sniffled and chuckled. "Sorry, baby girl, but you look gorgeous."

I linked my arm with hers as we turned to face the double doors that led out of the building I'd gotten ready in and out to where the ceremony was being held. Since we'd invited so many people to the public wedding, and neither of us was religious, we decided not to use a church. Instead, we were using a rose garden that we'd brought stadium seating in around the perimeter. None of the roses would be harmed; only the wedding party would be allowed inside the garden while the rest would be seated in the stands on the outside.

Stephan had hired a lot of extra security and cleared three blocks around to ensure no assassination attempts were made and no crazy women could try to interrupt the ceremony.

"Big breath, baby," Mom whispered.

I took a deep breath and Erina and Marlee nodded to the two guards in front of the doors. They were two of Erina's men, whose names still evaded me.

Erina and Marlee walked out and the doors shut again.

"You're sure about this? He may be nice and all, but he's still a rich guy who doesn't know what it's like to go a night without food," Mom asked.

I chuckled. "I'm sure, Mom."

She smiled and kissed my cheek. "I'm so glad you found happiness." She nodded at the guards who opened the doors again.

"Remember, those guys are the lucky ones," the one on the right whispered. "You are their goddess and they better treat you as such for the rest of your life."

"If they don't, Connor will let you live with us immediately," the one on the left said.

I snickered. "Thanks for the pep talk, boys."

"Just words of truth," they said and then stepped out behind me as we walked.

My eyes were immediately drawn to Stephan, who stood at the end of the walkway, beneath a wooden arch, wearing a tuxedo. He'd been staring at me, but his eyes snapped up to my face and he smiled, one of the purest and most loving smiles I had ever seen on his face.

Gasping in a breath, I let my mom lead me down the walkway.

To the left of Stephan stood my other men. Their eyes were full of varying emotions as they watched me walk towards them and I felt the same. Tomorrow, we would have our mafia wedding where I would marry all of them, even if it wasn't legally official.

"Breathe, girl. Breathe," she whispered out the side of her mouth as she continued to smile for all of the cameras.

I took a stuttering breath and returned Stephan's smile. In all of my life, I had never imagined I would have a wedding like this, that I would find love with men like them. Such amazing, cantankerous, protective, loving, and infuriating men.

We reached the end of our walk and Stephan stepped forward. Instead of taking my hand right away, he dropped to one knee and bowed his head.

The crowd murmured in shock, but my eyes were focused on Stephan.

He stood, kissed my mother's cheek, and then held his hand out to me. "My lady?"

I set my hand in his and let him walk me up to the officiant.

The ceremony blew by and before I knew it, Stephan and I had exchanged rings, said our "I do's", and kissed.

The crowd cheered and then an explosion of flashes went off as thousands of pictures were taken. Stephan and I posed for several photos, alternating between standing side-by-side smiling to cheek kisses or kisses on the lips. After a few minutes, he steered me to a waiting limousine.

The guys climbed in with us and then pulled away.

"Step one complete!" Arcadio cheered.

"Now for the food, booze, and dancing!" Dane said.

"Some of us get sprite," I reminded them.

"With cherries," Forrest said and winked.

I did love cherries in my drinks.

"You look amazing," Stephan said. "I couldn't say anything before, but this dress is superb. I couldn't have picked one as great as this."

"You have Erina to thank for that," I admitted. "Her designer is amazing."

Stephan squeezed our still joined hands. "You ready for the reception?"

"Not really," I admitted. "But I'm looking forward to dancing with you," I added quickly with a wide smile.

"Tomorrow is going to be even better," Shea said from the driver's seat.

"Jealous?" Stephan asked with a smirk.

"Yep," Shea admitted easily.

"Don't overdo it tonight," I ordered them all. "I don't want you puking on my dress tonight or unable to marry me tomorrow."

"Honey, we're not going to jeopardize our wedding," Forrest said and patted my leg.

"I'm so hungry," I complained. "How much farther is the reception site?"

"Fifteen minutes," Shea answered.

"Here," Arcadio said, pulled a granola bar from one of the compartments in the limo, as well as a plate, and held them out to me.

Tears pricked my eyes. "You brought me snacks and a plate so I wouldn't ruin my dress."

"Yes, we know you're much snackier lately," he said with a nod.

"I love you," I mumbled around the half of the granola bar I shoved into my mouth.

"We love you, too," Stephan said with an amused smirk.

Dane held out an opened water bottle. "Chew, Babe. Chew."

The reception went by uneventfully, but we ended up staying until well past midnight. Originally, we were going to stay at the old place, but the guys were worried about security concerns and the staff setting up for the wedding the next day, so we went to our new house. It was a gorgeous mansion and, thanks to me, well-fortified.

I'd changed out of my wedding dress at the reception site, under Erina's supervision, and put the dress into the garment bag before it was taken to go to the site for tomorrow's wedding. Once out of the dress, they'd allowed me to change into a light dress that was more like a slip, which allowed me to continue the night and still look pretty in pictures.

Stephan carried me into the house once we returned home

since I could barely walk on my own due to being so exhausted. "Although it wasn't the reason, I have now officially carried the bride over the threshold of our home."

I chuckled and kissed his neck. "What a wonderful husband."

"Don't you forget it," he murmured and nuzzled my hair. He didn't put me down in my room as I'd expected, instead he took me into his bedroom. "I'd like you to stay with me tonight, if that's alright with you?"

"What kind of wife would deny her newlywed husband on their wedding night?" I replied with a smile and then a massive yawn. I slapped a hand over my mouth. "Sorry."

He laughed as he untied his tie, removed his jacket, and shirt, and then turned to face me. "Don't apologize. We kept you out later than intended. You were great tonight, by the way. Smiling the entire time, even when that senator with the fish breath got in your face while talking to you. Thank you for not punching him, by the way."

"It was difficult, but I remembered to hold my breath." Kicking my shoes off, I slid beneath the covers, snuggling down until they were up to my neck and my head rested on one of his pillows.

Stephan crawled in behind me, spooned his body around mine, and hugged me. "I really am a lucky man," he whispered. "Finding someone I love, who loves me, but accepts my asexuality is not something I ever thought would happen. I always imagined this night would end with me having to sleep with the woman. To put on that façade to keep them with me."

"I hope you know that you never have to be anything other than yourself with me," I whispered and rubbed his forearm.

He squeezed me. "I know and I'm so glad that I have you."

"So, how many silver-and-diamond serving knives do you think we got?" I asked softly.

Stephan laughed and shook his head against my back. "Enough to make a serving set out of."

"We could melt them all down and make a throne," I suggested.

"That's not a bad idea," he chuckled. "Could you imagine other mafia leaders coming to see me and finding me sitting on a throne of silver-and-diamond serving knives?"

"Please do it," I begged.

He kissed the back of my head. "If there are seriously enough to do it, I will. Now, go to sleep, wife."

"Goodnight, husband."

The mafia wedding was definitely the most fun. By nine o'clock, everyone except Stephan and I were drunk. Connor and Brian kept making bets with Stephan and getting pissed when they lost.

"There's no way!" Brian yelled and slapped a hand on the top of the table. "How?"

Stephan smirked. "We all have our strengths, Torreto. Clearly, this isn't one of yours."

"There's no way you can beat me," Shea said and snorted.

"Bring it!" Blain, one of Erina's husbands, shouted and rolled the sleeves on his button-up shirt to his elbow.

Erina clutched my arm. "Oh, girl."

Shea did the same and I swallowed thickly. "I see, girl. I see."

Shea and Blain sat at one of the tables, elbows in the middle, which would have required me to lean across it, but both men were so large they were fully seated and able to do it.

"Kick his ass, Ox!" I shouted, egging him on and showing my support.

"Don't let him make you look weak!" Erina yelled at Blain. "Show these Moriarty men the might of the Gregori Mafia!"

Marlee sat down beside us, having returned from the restroom, and had her phone out to record immediately. "Oh, this is going to get good."

"Ready?" Shea asked, his hand clasped with Blain's.

Blain nodded, his shaved head reflecting the overhead lights. "Let's do this."

"Your Louboutin purse says my boy wins," Erina said.

"Your Coach purse says mine wins," I countered.

We looked at Marlee who shook her head. "I'm not betting on your guys. Besides, my husband has lost enough money tonight for the both of us."

I snickered and focused on the arm-wrestling competition before us.

"Three. Two. One," Forrest counted down beside them.

Shea and Blain's arms flexed as they pushed against each other, the veins on their necks bulged, and their eyes narrowed.

"Oh, hot!" Marlee said.

"Mine!" Erina and I shouted at the same time.

She giggled. "Yeah, yeah. I can still comment."

Shea and Blain's faces started turning red, but their hands hadn't moved.

"Are they evenly matched?" I asked Erina softly.

"That's surprising," she whispered.

It actually was because Blain wasn't as bulky as Shea or as

muscular in appearance, which meant his true strength was hidden. Scary.

"Mama needs a new purse!" I shouted at Shea.

Slowly, Shea started to push Blain's hand towards the table, but Blain shouted, and with a surge of strength, slammed Shea's hand into the tabletop. He stood and yelled victoriously.

I pouted and Erina patted my back. "That purse is going to look great with my new dress."

Shea rubbed his arm a moment, stood, and got right up in Blain's face.

Everyone tensed, preparing for a fight.

Shea glared a moment, then cracked a huge smile and held out his hand to shake Blain's. "You're stronger than you look."

Blain shook his hand and patted his back. "You, too!"

I thought the night might calm down, but then, the tattoo comparisons began and Erina, Marlee, and I were distracted by taking hundreds of photos as all of the guys removed their shirts.

"We could totally sell a calendar with these," I commented.

"Let's do it!" Erina said. "The guys don't even need to know."

"Are you kidding? If we put Stephan and Connor's names on it we'll get ten times as many orders!" I shouted.

"Oh, you're so right!" Marlee said. "Let's split the profits three ways and then we can buy that thing we discussed.

"What thing?" Stephan asked from behind us.

We all squealed.

"Nothing," Erina said quickly.

"Amelia," Stephan whispered in my ear. "What are you hiding?"

I spun around and scowled when I realized that he'd put his shirt back on.

"I'm not hiding anything. We discussed something that may never come to fruition, so it didn't have any merit to discuss with you," I said quickly.

"Hm," he replied, totally not buying my excuse.

"I can do fifty!" Arcadio shouted at Alexi.

"I can do a hundred!" Alexi shouted back.

"What are they talking about?" I asked Erina.

"How many push-ups they can do," she answered. "First to give up has to surrender a dagger!" she proposed, which got both of their attention as they were both assassins.

Arcadio and Alexi pulled their shirts off and dropped to their knees.

"Yes," I hissed into Erina's ear. "Best. Wedding. Ever."

"You're telling me," she mumbled. "I never get them to show off like this."

The two assassins started doing push-ups and I got lost staring at Arcadio's arms and upper back muscles.

"You're drooling," Dane whispered in my ear.

"Shush," I whispered. "Let me enjoy this."

By the end of the night, my stomach hurt from laughing so much and my face hurt from truly smiling so much.

Connor and Brian had to tear Marlee and Erina away from me when it came time to separate, but I promised them we'd spend time together soon. That seemed to pacify them at least long enough for their husbands to pull them away.

"Tonight was great," I whispered as Shea all but carried me to the SUV.

"I was skeptical before, but those two women really do love you," he whispered. "You seem…happier with them."

Rolling my head back to look up at the giant, I asked, "Does it make you jealous? You know I don't swing that way."

He chuckled. "No, but it makes me realize that it is important for you to have female friends. I take for granted having male friends because they're part of my family now. Seeing you with those two reminded me of how lucky I am."

"Aw, do you want to kiss, Ox?" Dane teased as he stumbled closer to us.

Shea held out his hand. "So help me, Crackers, I will knock you out if you try to kiss me."

Dane snickered and climbed into the SUV. "I love you, too."

"Oh, I won this for you," Stephan said and stepped away from the SUV before I climbed inside. He held out a folded piece of paper.

I took it warily, narrowing my eyes at him as I opened it. Both Connor and Brian and signed the document. It took me a moment to comprehend what I was reading. "Is...is this real? Binding?"

His smile grew as he nodded. "Yep. I had their seconds as witnesses to the signing before I won it."

In my hands was a signed agreement that turned the casino Connor and Brian co-owned in a shared territory into a triple-owned casino, with Stephan as the third owner.

"Does...what does this mean?" I asked, not wanting to get my hopes up.

"This means that there is now a place where you and your friends can go to spend time together that is neutral territory and owned by the three of us. So, your other husbands can't object to you wanting to go there." He smiled widely, so proud of himself.

Throwing my arms around him, he stumbled back a step

with a chuckle as I buried my face into his chest. "Thank you. Thank you so much. I don't know how I will ever repay you for this."

He wrapped his arms around me and kissed the top of my head. "Your happiness is all the payment I need. When I saw you three together tonight, and our men interacting so well, I knew this was something that needed to be done to further your happiness. Does it make you happy?"

"So fucking happy!" I screamed and hugged him tighter.

"Come on! Let's go home!" Forrest yelled, his words almost slurred together.

"Yes, it's time to get the drunkards home," Stephan said. He held open the passenger door for me.

"Are you driving?" I asked with wide eyes.

He looked at the others, nearly passed out in the middle and back seats. "You think they can drive?"

"Let me drive," I said and before he could protest, ran around to jump into the driver's seat.

"Amelia," he started, but sighed and climbed into the passenger seat. "I know there's no point in arguing, so we'll just say thank you."

"Thank you!" Arcadio, Shea, Dane, and Forrest chorused in various slurred voices.

I smiled so wide I swore my lips felt like they might tear. "You're welcome, husbands."

Yeah, I could definitely get used to that.

CHAPTER SIXTEEN

SEVERAL MONTHS LATER

"Oh!" I gasped and stood from the bed I'd been sitting on. What felt like a balloon sliding inside me suddenly popped and water gushed out, soaking my underwear and sweatpants. "My water broke!" I yelled.

Immediately, my five husbands ran into my room.

"Contractions?" Shea asked, the calmest of our group, though he hovered the closest.

"Not super strong, but I've been having them," I admitted. "Thought they were just more Braxton Hicks contractions since they weren't painful."

Stephan was on the phone immediately. "The doctor and his staff are on the way."

Mom walked into the room, wiping her hands on a hand towel, looking as relaxed as any other day. "Water broke?"

I nodded.

She smirked. "Oh, boy. Now the fun part begins."

I glared at her.

"Should we go to the hospital? Do we need a helicopter?" Shea asked her.

Mom patted his shoulder. "Easy, Shea. She's probably got another few hours before she needs to even start pushing the baby out. The doctor will get here long before she's ready to deliver."

"But her water—" he protested.

Mom patted his shoulder and instructed, "Deep breaths, honey. Take long, deep breaths. Even if the doctor doesn't show, I've delivered enough babies to handle it. My girl is strong and everything will be just fine. Why don't you go get some warm tea? It will help you calm down."

⸎

Mom had been right. It was another five hours before I actually needed to start pushing. Not that the pushing was anything to sniff at. I'd opted not to take medication and by the time I finished delivering, I was exhausted and glad it was over.

To our utter surprise, I'd actually been pregnant with twins.

Doc Octavius said it did happen sometimes that the twin hid behind the other and apologized profusely to Stephan. He looked legitimately terrified that Stephan might harm him or be upset.

Stephan was overjoyed, though, and didn't care since they were both healthy.

"I told you you weren't just getting fat," Mom said with a chuckle.

I narrowed my eyes. "You suspected I was pregnant with twins, didn't you?"

She nodded. "It runs in the family. Thankfully, it bypassed me, but most of the rest of the women in my family had twins."

I held my two sleeping babies against my chest and smiled down at them. The one on the left, my little girl, had dark hair that looked black but was hard to tell in the muted lights we had on. The one on the right, my little boy, had lighter brown hair. Both had blue eyes, but the doctor said they could change as they grew older.

"Good thing we overstocked on everything," Dane said softly as he came over to my side and rested a hand on the top of my head.

"Do you have names picked?" one of the nurses asked.

"Callen and Paige," I answered.

"Those are beautiful names," the nurse said.

"What last name are you giving them?" Mom asked.

"Moriarty," I answered immediately. "I'm legally married to Stephan and we aren't doing paternity tests on the babies."

"About that," the doctor said softly to Stephan. "I understand you don't care to know, but for medical reasons, it would be good for us to have medical backgrounds on their family. If you want, we can just get the medical backgrounds of all of the potential fathers and my office could discreetly run paternity tests so we can be sure to watch out for any potential issues. We don't have to disclose the results to anyone."

Stephan scowled as he thought about it. He looked at me. "What's your opinion on this?"

I shrugged. "Does it matter if we know who the actual

father is? Are any of you going to treat the children differently because you know it's not yours?"

"Of course not," Stephan said.

I smiled softly. "I know you won't. I was asking the others."

Shea shook his head. "I don't care if they are Dane's or Arcadio's. They are your children and that's what I care about."

"Same," Dane said.

"Agreed," Forrest said.

"Very well," Stephan said to the doctor.

"We don't want the answer," I said quickly. "You just keep it for the records."

He dipped his head. "Understood."

"How are you feeling?" Arcadio asked as he came to my side, brushing the back of his knuckles across my cheek.

"Tired," I admitted. "Happy."

"You should try to rest," he whispered. "We can take care of the babies while you sleep."

"You should all try skin-to-skin with the babies if you're willing," Doc said. "It will help them remember your smells."

Arcadio whipped his shirt off and held out his hands. "Let me hold Callen. Dane can take Paige. We know how to hold babies and can feed them a bottle if they get hungry."

"We also know how to change diapers," Dane added.

"Sleep does sound good," I admitted as I relinquished my babies.

Dane and Arcadio held the babies against their chests like seasoned pros, and both began talking to them in soft, kind tones.

Stephan hovered at my side, as did Shea. Forrest and Mom followed Dane and Arcadio, trying to take the babies from them.

I knew, without a doubt, that these babies would be spoiled and never left wanting.

The next few weeks spun by in a hurricane of diapers, bottles, and adorableness.

Erina and Marlee came to visit, cooing over the babies and fawning over me.

I sat in a recliner, watched my two best female friends, both mafia queens, sway back and forth with my twins in their arms, and felt joy fill me until I started crying.

Stephan, who'd barely left my side since I'd given birth, just walked into the room and rushed over to me. "What's wrong? Are you in pain? Do I need to call the doctor?"

I smiled and shook my head. "I'm just so happy. I've got more than I ever could have wished for in my life."

An explosion sounded and then an alarm blared.

Instantly, I was up out of my recliner, the shotgun I kept in the side of it in my hands and ready.

Marlee and Erina stared at me with wide eyes.

"Damn, girl," Erina said. "You're faster than my boys."

I winked. "That's the only time it's a positive to hear that."

She snorted, which made little Paige fuss. Erina quickly cooed and bounced her in her arms to quiet her again.

Stephan pulled out his tablet and tapped into the security footage. At the edge of our property stood a tall man with a handlebar mustache. He had his arms raised as he looked up into the camera. The explosion had been the net launcher over our front door shooting to try to snag him. He'd somehow dodged it.

"Can I help you?" Shea asked through the intercom system.

"I'm here to see my daughter," the man said.

I looked at Erina and Marlee who both shook their heads.

Stephan looked at me and glanced at Paige.

My eyes narrowed into a glare. "Don't you even think it, *husband*. I haven't cheated on you guys."

"Your daughter?" Shea asked.

"Amelia," he said. "I'm Amelia's father."

I pulled my cell phone from my pocket, video-called my mother and turned the phone so she could see the security footage.

She cursed and broke something. "So, he is alive. Keep him there until I can make it so I can kill his ass!"

I hung up and nodded at Stephan. "Let him in."

He sent a text to Shea who walked down the road to escort the man in.

"Can you two stay here with the babies unless I call you in?" I asked Erin and Marlee.

Erina tapped her lower back. "We're packing, baby. I'll blast anyone who tries to get in this room."

Marlee nodded at my shotgun. "Leave it on the recliner. And remember to knock correctly this time."

"You forgot! Not me!" I shouted as I set the gun down, safety on. "Three, two, one."

She rolled her eyes. "Yeah. Yeah. At least you got a cool scar out of it."

The brat had shot me in the arm, just a graze thankfully because she swore I missed one of the knocks in our pattern. I hadn't, but I wasn't really mad at her about it anymore.

After kissing Paige and Callen on the heads, I left them in the arms of two highly dangerous women and followed Stephan to our reception room.

Shea, Dane, Forrest, and Arcadio stood around the room, eyes focused on the man who sat on the love seat.

He was taller than I expected, eyes the same color as mine,

but hair much lighter. When I entered with Stephan, he stood and smiled. "You look just like your momma."

"Why are you here? Now?" I asked.

"You look familiar," Stephan commented and looked at Forrest. "Who is he?"

"I'm Amelia's biological father. Originally, I was part of her mother's polyamorous harem, but when shit hit the fan, I had to fake my own death and go into hiding," he said.

"Holy shit," Forrest whispered as he walked over and held out his tablet to Stephan. "You're Stanley Marvél."

My mouth dropped. "Serious?" Stanley Marvél was a renowned mafia boss who had dominated half of the East Coast, took over most of the industries, and even had the cops on his payroll. His death and disappearance were something widely discussed and researched with no answers.

Stanley, my biological father, sighed. "I shouldn't be surprised you figured that out so fast. Yes, I am."

All eyes turned to me.

"That means you're the heir to the Marvél fortune," Dane whispered.

"I'm sorry…the what?" I asked.

Stanley smiled. "When I *died* and disappeared, my fortune disappeared with me. It's been in an offshore account, waiting for me to find you."

"I wasn't exactly hiding," I muttered. "Mom knew where I was."

He flinched. "My past started catching up with me, so I had to die again."

"How many times have you died?" I asked.

"Not too many yet," he said with a chuckle.

"Why are you here now?" I asked.

"I saw your wedding on the news," he said with a soft

smile. "I'd thought that if I wasn't part of your life that you'd be able to live normally, have the white picket fence and all that. Had I known you'd just end up in the arms of a mafia boss, I would have intervened sooner."

"Intervening wouldn't have worked," Mom said as she entered the room. "She's more stubborn than you are."

He flinched and turned to look at her. "You're even more lovely than the last time I saw you."

She walked up to him, punched him on the jaw, and glared. "You son of a bitch! I thought you were dead. I cried. I mourned for years!"

Instead of backing away—or giving any other response I might've anticipated—he threw his arms around her. "I'm so sorry, my beautiful love. If it helps, I never forgot you and never took another lover after I left you."

Why were tears building in my eyes at that?

She sniffled. "I hate you."

He nodded against her hair. "You should."

"I tortured so many people looking for you," she whispered.

"She really is just like her mom," Dane whispered to Forrest.

Instead of rising to the bait of his statement, I stepped forward and hugged both of my biological parents.

They dropped an arm from each other to hug me, pulling me into my first ever biological family hug.

"Why are you here?" I asked once we finally pulled back. "I don't mean to sound callous, but—"

"A father should give his daughter a wedding present. Plus, I wanted to meet my grandchildren," he said. He looked at Stephan. "I've not been in the game for over two decades now. Please, let me meet my grandchildren and make up for lost time with my daughter. I will sign whatever agreements you want. Pay you whatever you want. Please. Let me have my white picket time with her before I die."

The way he said it had my mind racing. Was he ill? Or was he just well aware of how fragile life could be as a mafia boss and leader?

"Elizabeth Sarah, may I speak to you outside?" Stephan asked.

Mom pulled herself away from Stanley to follow Stephan outside.

"You seem to be doing well?" Stanley commented with a soft smile.

I nodded. "I lucked into finding these hooligans and couldn't be happier."

"I'm going to update the girls," Shea said in a whisper as he walked by me and towards the exit.

"Don't forget the knock!" I shouted at his retreating back.

He raised a single thumbs-up to me as he left.

"Why'd you quit?" Forrest asked bluntly. "Your mafia was one of the biggest. You were renowned. A legend!"

"I wanted a family," he told Forrest. "Sure, I had plenty of women I could spend my nights with. Plenty who threw themselves at me. It isn't the same, though. I ran away, hid in a small town in the middle of nowhere. I wanted to escape, to find some breathing room for a bit, but ended up finding love. Eli was a spitfire, a tornado with luscious curves and a mouth that could cut glass. She didn't know who I was, didn't care, and treated me like an equal. It was a nice reprieve from the life I had been living. Being a mafia boss comes with a lot of trivial, monotonous tasks. Some of which include dealing with disputes on your territory between your lieutenants. Eli showed me another way to live. I faked my death to have a life with her, but my second came after me and the only way to keep the love of my life safe was to once again fake my death. This time, I had to make it look as real as possible and not come back. I didn't know she was pregnant." He turned to me. "Had I known she was carrying you, I would have done things differently. I'm glad you had your other fathers to raise you, but I regret not being there for you. You're my only daughter and I don't want to miss out on my grandchildren's lives. I want to experience it as I should in my old age. I know that you don't know me from Adam, and I will do whatever you want to prove myself to you."

Mom and Stephan had come into the room quietly during his explanation and Mom's eyes were misty.

"You should have told me," she whispered.

He spun around. "I'm sorry, love. I couldn't. I did it to protect you...and even though I didn't know it, her."

"If I allow you to be part of our family, you can't disappear again," I whispered. "My children are going to be raised in a mafia family. They will be in danger whether you exist or not, so you don't get to use that danger as an excuse."

He nodded. "I won't run away. If something happens, I'll talk to Stephan and ask for his help. As much as it pains me to even think about asking someone for help, for you and my grandchildren, I will."

Stephan smiled. "It seems we're family now, so of course I would offer you aid."

"Can you draft something real quick?" I asked Stephan.

He looked at Forrest. "Alliance form?"

Forrest nodded, tapped on his screen a bit, and then held the tablet out to Stephan.

Stephan read the document over, nodded, and held it out

to Stanley. "Sign an alliance agreement with me and we can introduce you to your grandchildren."

Stanley took the offered tablet, read through the entire document, and then signed. After he handed the tablet back to Stephan, he clapped and rubbed his hands together, smiled wide, and asked, "Where are my grandbabies?"

⚓

As Stanley and Mom played with their grandbabies, I relaxed on the couch with my two best friends. Marlee and Erina had turned on a true crime documentary to try and guess which of the groups had done it. Shortly thereafter, all of my guys had gathered to add their guesses in, too, and then money started getting tossed onto the coffee table as they made wagers on who was right.

Forrest's phone rang as he leaned against the front of the couch between my legs, and he answered it without checking the caller ID. "Hello?"

As soon as the person spoke, he straightened and his entire body went rigid.

"I thought you were dead," he whispered.

Erina paused the show and everyone turned to look at him.

Forrest stood and began pacing back and forth in front of the television. "I know. Yeah, I remember. I know!" The last words were a roar and his free hand clenched into a fist at his side. "I understand. Yes. Yes, I'll be there."

Before I'd thought it, I was on my feet and walking to him.

He hung up the phone, looked over at Stephan, and said, "The Toupee is calling in his favor from me."

Stephan groaned and let his head drop back. "I thought he'd died."

"The Toupee as in Torrence Malone? Of the Malone Mafia?" Erina asked.

Forrest nodded then looked down at me and smiled. "Looks like we'll be checking off another item from your bucket list. We're going to Scotland in six months."

My eyes widened. "Scotland? I've always wanted to visit! We get to see a castle, right? We *have* to see a castle! I'll kick and scream until I see one."

Erina and Marlee chuckled behind me.

"We're going to see my castle, promise," Stephan said behind me with a chuckle. "No need to kick and scream."

"Spoilsport," I whispered.

That had everyone laughing and once again, my heart felt full.

THE STORY CONTINUES...

To find out what happens next, check out Suddenly Baroness, the next book in the Accidental Mobster Series.

CONNECT WITH CATHERINE BANKS

I really appreciate you reading my book! I hope you enjoyed it.

Please consider leaving a review at your favorite site.

Here are some ways to connect with me:

www.catherinebanks.com

Follow me on BookBub: https://www.bookbub.com/authors/catherine-banks

Join my Patreon: http://www.patreon.com/catherinebanks

Purchase items handmade by Catherine: http://Etsy.com/shop/TurboKittenInd

ABOUT THE AUTHOR

Catherine Banks is a USA Today bestselling fantasy author who writes in several fantasy subgenres and has multiple pseudonyms. She began writing fiction at only four years old and finished her first full-length novel at the age of fifteen. She is married to her soulmate and best friend, Avery, who she has two amazing children with. After her full-time job, she reads books, plays video games, and watches anime shows and movies with her family to relax. Although she has lived in Northern California her entire life, she dreams of traveling around the world. Catherine is also C.E.O. of Turbo Kitten Industries™, a company with many hats including being a book publisher and Etsy store full of nerdy fun.

facebook.com/catherinebanksauthor
twitter.com/catherineebanks
amazon.com/author/catherinebanks
bookbub.com/authors/catherine-banks

MORE FROM CATHERINE BANKS

YOUNG ADULT PARANORMAL & FANTASY ROMANCE SERIES

Artemis Lupine Series
Song of the Moon
Kiss of a Star
Healed by the Fire
Battles of the Night
Artemis Lupine, The Complete Series

Little Death Bringer Duology
Mercenary
Protector
Little Death Bringer, The Official Coloring Book

Pirate Princess Series
Pirate Princess
Princess Triumvirate

ADULT PARANORMAL & FANTASY ROMANCE SERIES

Zodiac Shifters Paranormal Romance Series

Centaur's Prize

Tiger Tears

Lion About

Ciara Steele Novella Series

True Faces

Barbaric Tendencies

ADULT REVERSE HAREM PARANORMAL & FANTASY ROMANCE SERIES

Her Royal Harem Series

Royally Entangled

Royally Exposed

Royally Elected

Royally Enraged

Her Royal Harem, The Complete Series

The Demon's Fair

Her Royal Harem, The Coloring Book

Wings of Vengeance Series

Of Dragons and Cruelty

Of Minotaurs and Sacrifice

Wings of Vengeance, The Complete Series

Anderelle: Minloa Trilogy

Queen of the Stars

Empress of the Galaxy

Goddess of the Universe

Anderelle: Minloa, The Complete Series

Bonds of Madness Series
Sealing the Deal
Racing the Clock

Her Super Harem Series
Lucky Strike

VELLA ADULT PARANORMAL REVERSE HAREM ROMANCE
Shark (Season One)

*Coming Soon

MORE FROM CATHERINE BANKS

STANDALONE YOUNG ADULT PARANORMAL & FANTASY ROMANCE BOOKS

Monster Academy

Daughter of Lions

Lady Serra and the Draconian

Of Sky and Sea

The Last Werewolf

Sybil Deceived

An Outcast Among Wolves

STANDALONE YOUNG ADULT PARANORMAL & FANTASY REVERSE HAREM ROMANCE BOOKS

Moon Academy

STANDALONE ADULT PARANORMAL & FANTASY ROMANCE BOOKS

Demonic Contract

Anja's Secret

Dragon's Blood

Last Ama Princess

Transforming Rose

Alys of Asgard

Phoenix Possessed

Stone Heart

STANDALONE URBAN FANTASY BOOKS

The Pawn

CHILDREN'S BOOKS

Calvin's Alien Adventure

MORE FROM DAISY EMORY

The Boyfriend Deal

Their Purple Girl

Courting Love

ACCIDENTAL MOBSTER SERIES
Accidental Mobster
Unintentional Pirate
Suddenly Baroness
Unexpected Assassins*

*Coming Soon